The Last Thylacine

Terry Domico

Turtleback Books
Friday Harbor, Washington
Sydney, Australia

The Last Thylacine

Turtleback Books
Post Office Box 2012
Friday Harbor, Washington
98250 USA

Turtleback Books
Attn: J. Vaughan
18 Myee Avenue
Strathfield, NSW
2135 Australia

For Ordering Information:
Please contact Turtleback Books at *turtlebackbooks@usa.com* or in Australia *turtlebackbooks@australiamail.com* Quantity purchase discounts are available.

Domico, Terry (1946-)
> The Last Thylacine / Terry Domico;
> Includes glossary of selected Australian and technical terms.

ISBN 1-883385-15-6

10 9 8 7 6 5 4 3 2 1   Printed in the USA

To Mark, who inspired this book,
and Kelly, who enthusiastically
listened as the story
revealed itself.

*

*

Other Fine (Nonfiction) Books by
Internationally Acclaimed Nature
Writer and Photographer
Terry Domico

Wild Harvest

Bears of the World

Kangaroos: The Marvelous Mob

The Nature of Borneo (Photography)

*

The Last Thylacine

PART ONE

Chapter One

After about twenty minutes, the female stood up and began tearing bits of flesh from the wallaby carcass. Since the pups had successfully scavenged quite a bit of meat on their own, they did not ravenously gobble the pieces their mother provided them. Matthew was sure this was a signal that the weaning process was almost over.

All of a sudden, both pups and parents dashed into the den. Since he hadn't moved a muscle, Matthew also knew that it wasn't he who had frightened them. Expecting to see another eagle attack, he leaned forward in hopes of catching a glimpse of it. What he saw made his heart sink; no eagle had scared those animals, it was a man.

Victor stood with his hands on his hips and feet spread apart in a attitude of defiance.

"Matthew!" he roared. "You son of a bitch! You've been holding out on us."

Matthew climbed out of the observation hide and walked up to him, face to face.

"It's not what you think, Victor, I was going to tell you about my discovery as soon as I'd had a chance to learn a bit more about them. I've already more than doubled the world's knowledge about how these

1

animals live."

"Bull shit! We're here to trap the damned
things. What if they had run away while you were busy
'studying' them?" Victor retorted.

"It was a risk that I was willing to take,"
Matthew replied.

"You bastard, you're risking more than four
months of our hard work, not to mention the reward
I was promised," Victor exclaimed.

"Well, Victor, now that you know about them,
we might as well catch..."

Matthew was unable to finish his sentence
before a crashing blow from Victor's fist smacked him in
the face and knocked him to the ground.

"So that's how you want it, eh?"

Matthew quickly got back on his feet and took
a swing at Victor. He ducked and landed another blow,
on the chin this time. Matthew held his ground.

"I don't want to fight you, Victor."

"Tough shit!"

Victor parried two of Matthew's jabs and then
struck him squarely. Still holding his ground, Matthew
swung again and caught him just below the right ear.
That blow must have really hurt because Victor came
back like a madman.

Matthew landed two more good hits. With
each blow, however, Victor seemed to grow in strength.
A flurry of punches knocked Matthew to the ground
once more. As he attempted to regain his feet, Victor
kicked him in the head and he fell unconscious.

When Matthew awoke, the sun was well on its way towards the noon apex. He estimated that he must have been out for at least an hour. His left eye was swollen closed and his head was racked with pain. He was unable to sit properly, let alone stand up. Victor was nowhere to be seen. The animals that he had worked so hard to observe were also gone; he wondered if he would ever see them again.

"Damn, my head hurts. I've got a loose tooth, too," he muttered to himself.

Crawling back to his tent, he encountered his belongings, dumped on the ground in a scattered array. He picked up the first-aid kit and a water bottle and then crept into the tent. After washing the dried and clotted blood from his face, he applied a dressing to the gash over his eyebrow and stretched out on his sleeping bag. It was evening before he woke again.

As he sat and waited for daylight to return, the events of the past year and a half tumbled over and over in his mind. Like most things, it had begun rather innocently.

...

At forty-two years of age, Matthew Clark was enjoying a scientific career with a reputation for being one of the most successful freelance field-biologists in Australia, specializing in environmental and wildlife assessment work. As anyone who freelances knows, full-time employment - even for a few months at a time - is infrequent and very difficult to secure. But the

3

scheduling and responsibility for completion for each project that Matthew was hired to do was strictly his and he liked it that way.   Usually he worked alone, truly enjoying his outback solitude, with Nature as his only companion.

This story began while he was finishing the tenth month of a yearlong contract to complete a biological survey of a proposed addition to the Lake Saint Clair National Park in the highlands of central Tasmania. Parts of this densely forested alpine region are so rugged that they have probably never been visited before, even by trappers and prospectors.

It was hoped by his employer, the Tasmanian Parks and Wildlife Department, that this half million acre addition of open savanna and dense bush, collectively known as the "Great Pine Tier," would qualify this wilderness as an UNESCO World Heritage Site.

It was also hoped, by the region's influential tourist industry, that this classification would focus some attention on Australia's smallest state, Tasmania. The recent slump in Australia's economy had hit this island particularly hard and he was grateful to have work, especially when he'd been seeing his colleagues taking odd jobs in order to make ends meet.

During a storm one night, a sudden rush of wind had swept into Matthew's tent, flipping the canvas door back onto the roof. For a few moments, a scattering of oversized drops drummed the ceiling. Then the rain came in wind-driven torrents.

4

Half awake, he had rolled over in his snug sleeping-bag. A sheath of papers left unguarded on a camp stool slipped to the floor as a gust of rain-laden wind spattered his face, provoking him to sit up with a start.

"Jeeeeze," Matthew muttered in the darkness, "this weather is sure lousy... I'd better close that entry... otherwise, I'll be up to my butt in water by daybreak."

Thrusting his hand out from under cover, he felt in the darkness for the electric torch.

Got it.

Bright light illuminated streaks of rain in the tent's doorway. Matthew reluctantly crawled out of his warm nest and stuck his head out into the storm.

There'll probably be snow on the mountain pass. I'll bet it's an early winter this year

Sticking the handle of the torch into his mouth, Matthew grabbed at the fluttering end of the canvas, pulled the door back inside, and began zipping it closed.

"She's <u>really</u> a wild night!" he mumbled out loud to himself as he turned his head to sweep the light's beam over his solitary wilderness camp. The steel cooking tripod had blown over and a large branch swayed crazily overhead. Then he saw it.

What the hell is that?

The light briefly illuminated a yellowish dog-like animal that stood as still as a statue next to where the cooking fire had burned earlier that night. Letting go of the door, which was instantly flipped back again by the wind, he removed the torch from his

5

mouth and carefully spotlighted the creature for a better look.

"A Thylacine! Well, I'll be... they really do exist!" he breathed soundlessly. Instinctively, he had automatically lapsed into the silent manner of a hunter.

The circle of light revealed a row of dark stripes along the animal's back that ran part way down its sides and haunches. Unperturbed, it continued to stand and gaze serenely at the source of the light, blinking only when drops of rain splashed into its eyes.

Two thoughts formed simultaneously in Matthew's mind, *Thylacines are supposed to be extinct!* and *I must get a photo!*

Holding the light steadily on the collie-sized creature, he groped through his belongings with his free hand.

Where's that bloody camera? There it is...
Oh no! I forgot to remove that old roll of exposed film.

His hands shaking with excitement and frustration, Matthew shifted the torch again to his mouth, trying to keep it fixed on the subject while his hands fumbled in the dark. After he had wound the film back into its cassette, he released the camera's back and plucked the film out, dropping it in his haste to the muddy ground.

Damn!

Rain splashed the exposed shutter mechanism and pooled in the low spots of the camera's interior.

Matthew popped open a fresh film canister with his left hand and tried to align the cassette in the

6

camera. However, the slight "pop" sound of the canister caused the animal to flinch and stiffen to attention.

Oh no! It's going to leave!

As if responding to his thoughts, the Thylacine wheeled about and trotted off into the night.

"My God...!" Matthew gasped, letting the now forgotten camera drop into the mud alongside the rewound film cassette. His mind was numb with the shock of recognition of what he had just witnessed. All of his life he had seen those same antique photos which accompanied nearly every newspaper story that reported another so-called Thylacine sighting: "The Tasmanian 'tiger' syndrome," he had called them. For Matthew Clark, up until a moment ago, the last Thylacine in the world had died in the Hobart Zoo back in 1936.

The Thylacine, also known as the Tasmanian tiger, was (or is) the world's largest marsupial carnivore. It looks a bit like a dog with a large head, short legs, and a stiff kangaroo-like tail.

Males, more solidly built than the females, weigh up to seventy-five pounds and measure nearly two feet high at the shoulder. Both sexes share the species' most distinctive feature: a series of fifteen to twenty black to dark brown tiger-like stripes running across the back from the shoulders to the base of the tail. Being a marsupial - more closely related to kangaroos than dogs - the female Thylacine also has a pouch. Unlike a kangaroo's pouch, this one opens towards the rear so that it won't snag on twigs, branches, or other obstacles when it runs through the bushland. A mother Thylacine can carry up to four small pups in her pouch at a time, but when they grow too large, she often hides them in a lair when she goes hunting.

This is primarily a nocturnal species and it normally hunts in the evening or at night, usually alone but sometimes in pairs. Using its acute sense of smell, a Thylacine can tirelessly track a fleeing wallaby to exhaustion, then kill and eat what it wants. When weaned, the young are sometimes allowed to follow the hunt and feed on the remains.

Thylacines were never very numerous in Tasmania and they were quite shy of humans. Unfortunately, they were also very fond of mutton, as the early settlers of Tasmania soon discovered. In 1835, a bounty for killing them was introduced and during the next seventy-five years, more than three thousand of the animals were destroyed. By 1910, the end was in sight; over the next twenty years the Tasmanian tiger virtually disappeared.

Since 1936, when the last known Thylacine died, researchers have spent hundreds of thousands of dollars looking for some conclusive evidence of the animal's continued existence. Although scientific results from these efforts have been absolutely zero, there have been more than four hundred Tasmanian tiger sightings reported in just the past twenty years by a wide variety of people, including farmers, hunters, woodsmen... even school teachers on vacation from England. Nevertheless, since not one of those individuals could produce any hard evidence of their experience in the form of photographs or tracks, all of their testimonies had been completely discounted by the scientific community. Matthew's own attitude on this matter, however, had just been abruptly changed.

Peering intently into the dark storm, he huddled in the opening of his tent for the remainder of the night. He managed to ignore his aching legs while his breathing, deep and regular, seemed to expand his focused senses beyond this small camp, past the grassy shoulder of the nearby hill, and down into the narrow forested valley that stretched away before him in the darkness.

Slowly, with infinite gradualness, the rains sputtered to a stop and a reddened blush of approaching dawn appeared on the horizon of a partly cleared sky. The Thylacine had not returned.

Chapter Two

As he lifted his heavy backpack and slipped its straps over his shoulders, Matthew realized that he had just two more months in which to complete the park assessment project. Then he would be seeking new work. He wondered if the past four days that he had spent looking for another glimpse or sign of the Thylacine had been worth the effort. After an intense search, often on his hands and knees, he had found nothing. Every trace of the animal had been completely erased by the storm.

Ahead of him was the three and a half day hike back to the dirt road at Nive River where his battered four-wheel-drive Land Cruiser was parked. A few hours drive would then take him to Hobart where he planned to announce the Thylacine sighting to his superiors at the Department.

"Certainly Roger Garvey, the project leader, would believe me," he told himself.

Perhaps he could even swing an additional contract to search for the elusive animal. Since he was the person most familiar with the back country of this proposed addition to the park... and a verified sighting of a Tasmanian tiger... well, that would be the icing that confirmed the park's World Heritage status. Roger would love that. He was constantly bugging the press to do more coverage on the plans for the park and what it would mean to Tasmania's tourism.

"Roger? It's Matthew here," he announced after the secretary had put his telephone call through. "A'rright if you meet me for a cupper this morning, mate? Something's come up that we had best discuss."

"What is it?" Roger queried. "You weren't supposed to be back here for another fortnight. Everything okay?"

"Well... it's something that I would rather talk to you about in person, Roger. Are you free to go out for coffee in about an hour?"

Roger was beginning to get impatient. Matthew was usually more straight to the point. "Can't you tell me what it's about? What... did you find some young lass in your camp bed when you woke up this morning?"

"C'mon! It's serious... I'll tell you about it when we get together. Meet me at the coffee shop near the office in an hour?"

"Okay, mate... See you in a bit."

...

With both hands wrapped around a cup of steaming brew, Roger listened in silence as Matthew related his story. After he had finished, Roger remained quiet for a few moments, as if weighing all of its ramifications.

"Fair dinkum? Are you sure that's what you saw, man?" he asked.

"Absolutely!"

"Matt, do you realize what this means? Why,

12

we could really be on the map! Imagine... a live
Tasmanian tiger... or better yet, a family of them...
That would sure bring the tourists over! It could be
good for the Department's operating budget as well."

"Roger, I think we should put a few people
together and go back and do a dedicated search until we
find the animal, or at least some definite sign of its
existence."

"Huh?... Right!" agreed Roger, somewhat
absently. His mind was already spinning with new
plans.

"Listen, Matthew... Can you come up to my
office after lunch? Say around 3:00 PM? I'll have some
people there who you can talk to about this."

"Certainly."

Getting up from the table, Roger bid a lively,
"Right-o! Matt... see you then," and plunged into the
vivacious crowd waiting at the doorway. Although
seating was limited, this was one of the most popular
meeting places in town.

As Matthew finished his last few swallows of
coffee, he began to feel elated. Maybe it had been a
good idea after all to break the survey trip and come
back with this news. Most likely it would be he who
would be chosen to head any study team assigned to the
area where he had seen the Thylacine. Why, he might
even be able to hire a couple of his friends who were
excellent bush trackers, but not so competent at finding
work.

At 2:58 PM, Matthew arrived at Roger Garvey's

office. The outer door was open and voices filled the hallway as he approached. Roger's best public-relations smile greeted him when Matthew entered the room. Newspaper and TV reporters surrounded him.

"Why, here's the man of the hour now!"

Matthew was stunned. Roger had already called a press conference and was waiting for him to deliver the glowing report.

"For Christ-sake, Roger, this is no time to talk to the bloody press; the whole thing is premature!" was all he could blurt out. Shaken by the surprise, he turned to leave.

One of the television reporters stepped forward and demanded angrily, "What is this? Some sort of put-on? This Parks and Wildlife bureaucrat pulls us out of a busy schedule and promises us proof that the Tasmanian tiger still exists and you're just going to leave us standing here like dopes? What's the story?"

"The story is... that there is nothing to talk about!" Matthew hastily replied. "I'm sorry you've been called over here on a wild goose chase. I'm afraid that you've been misinformed."

Nearly everyone in the whole room shot an annoyed glance at Roger. Then almost as a single unit, the people of the press began to leave. In less than a minute, Roger and Matthew stood alone, facing each other.

"Damn it, man! You blew our big chance!" Roger exclaimed.

"You had no right..." Matthew retorted

defensively. "You could have at least waited until we had some real proof before you went into your grand promotion routine."

"No right! Hey man, I'm your boss!"

"That is an unfortunate situation!" Matthew replied and made for the door. "See ya later, _mate_."

On the way home, Matthew fumed and considered how quickly these recent events had taken a wrong turn. However, by the time he had parked the car in his driveway, he had regained his normal composure.

When not out in the "bush," Matthew lived in a modest house located near downtown Hobart, the island state's capital city. After his wife died from leukemia nearly two years ago, he stayed alone here mostly buried in his work, seldom seeing friends, and even more rarely visited by his nineteen-year-old son Brian.

I hope Roger comes to his senses over this, he thought as he opened the front door. Just as he stepped inside, his telephone began to ring.

"Hello?"

"Mr. Clark?" a young man's voice asked.

"Yes?"

"Mr. Clark, my name is Brad Lewis... I'm the secretary of the director of the National Parks and Wildlife Department."

"_Yes_?" A note of caution began to creep into Matthew's voice.

"Mr. Clark, we have been reviewing our

contract with you and have recently discovered that the Department is experiencing a serious budgetary shortfall. In brief, sir, we are forced to ask you not to send us your regular monthly progress report and to discontinue for an indefinite period your assistance on the Lake Saint Clair Annex project."

"What the..." Matthew began to answer and then he caught himself. "Oh, I see..." It was impossible to argue with this kind of bureaucratic double-talk.

"If there is a financial surplus in the Department during the next fiscal term," the voice continued, "we'll call you. All right?"

What could he say? All Matthew could manage was to mutter a croaked "Thank you."

After hanging up the telephone receiver, he stared at his neatly ordered desk and drummed his fingers on a reference book about aquatic plants. Picking up a specimen bottle, he examined it in the strong glare of his reading light.

"No more work... no more work," he repeated slowly to himself. Roger had worked surprisingly fast.

The following weeks were painfully tedious. Matthew spent several hours each day sitting at that old wooden desk tapping his forefinger and staring, lost in thought. He was trying to determine what his next move should be. Should he go to the mainland and look for work? Or should he stay here and tough it out? He knew if he stayed, the best he could look forward to would be a few small-time freelance jobs in the private sector. He probably would have to find another line of work that would support him.

Each night he drank half a six-pack of beer to help blur his concentration and fall asleep. Sometimes though, he would wake in the middle of the night to find himself still sitting at his desk, slumped over his now useless field notes from the Lake Saint Clair Annex.

As he concentrated his energy into self-examination and perhaps self-pity, Matthew began to neglect his appearance. He stopped shaving, rarely took a shower or even changed his clothes. Sometimes, he hardly noticed whether it was light or dark outside or even if he was hungry. His preoccupied mind was working on the problem of what to do... few biology careers ever survived black-listing by Parks and Wildlife, or any other government agency, for that matter.

Little by little, Matthew slipped into a roller-coaster of self-doubt and depression. After two months marked by daily bouts of resignation punctuated by brief flurries of frantic, almost manic activity, he received more bad news.

Laura had been the love of his life and they were in the full bloom of their marriage when she was struck down by the cancer. She had fought the fatal illness bravely, but when the ordeal finally ended, it had left Matthew emotionally drained and economically tied to an enormous debt for medical expenses. To help pay off this burden, he had taken out a second mortgage on his house... their house. He was now several months

17

in arrears with his payments.

The letter from the bank's loan officer threatened to foreclose on the mortgage if Matthew didn't bring his account up to date immediately.

"I can give you an allowance until the end of the month," she had said when Matthew telephoned to explain his circumstances. "That's the best I can do."

Pulling his resources together, Matthew gravely discovered that he could only muster half of the required amount. This was no good. His depression continued to deepen into dreary hopelessness.

Then it happened. One morning, while frying eggs for breakfast and looking for a clean dish in the cluttered pile in the sink, he came to a decision. The idea had come suddenly and its sudden flash, like a match struck in a dark room, clearly revealed the details of the contents. Matthew slammed down the pan, turned off the stove and marched back to his desk. Picking up the telephone receiver and an address book, he began dialing old acquaintances. His eyes narrowed into a sense of purpose. By tea-time he had logged over a dozen calls, several of them overseas.

The next afternoon, a big motorcycle rumbled up Matthew's driveway, rattling the windows of the small house. The bang of the back door being slammed was immediately followed by a call of "Hey Dad!" as his son Brian pulled off his helmet, unzipped his leather jacket, and wandered into the kitchen. With thick sandy hair and blue eyes, Brian was a ruggedly handsome young man who enjoyed the "biker" image.

He wore a death's head tattoo on his right arm and a gold ring in his left ear. A red bandanna covered his head. Intelligent and soft-spoken when off-guard, Brian normally tried to maintain a rebellious manner. That "tough guy" image, however, seemed just slightly too assumed to ever become hardened and real.

"Phew! What a mess," Matthew heard him exclaim at the pile of dirty dishes, half-eaten meals, and empty beer bottles. "Whadd-ya got to eat?" he queried as he pulled open the refrigerator. "Jeese...not much," he winced as he answered his own question. "Dad? You around?"

Matthew was busy drafting a letter when Brian entered the study. This room had become central to his existence and was the only place in the house that was kept clean and orderly.

"Hi Dad."

"Huh? Oh hello... How yer doing?"

"Good-nuff."

"How's the bike running?"

"A'rright. Heard that you got fired."

"The Department says that it's just 'temporary'."

"From the look of things around here, Dad, we both know that's not true. Is it?"

"Yeah... you're right. How're you and that new girl friend of yours getting along?"

"Not-so-good." After a short pause Brian added, "Dad, how 'bout loaning me some money? I'm broke."

"How about you looking for a job, Brian?" he answered. "You haven't lifted a finger to help yourself in over a year and a half. You expect me to carry you forever? Look... you've insisted on living on your own ever since your mother passed away... why don't you stop shacking up with every girl you meet and start doing something for yourself?"

Even as Matthew said these things, he realized that he was being unfairly hard on his son. But he was angry at the whole world at that moment and didn't feel the least bit apologetic.

"Doing something for myself?" Brian retorted, "Jesus... Look at this mess you live in. You ought to take your own bloody advice and get with it!"

With that comment, Brian turned and hotly left the room, went down the hall and through the kitchen, grabbing his helmet off the table on his way. Once again the back door slammed and a moment later the roar of his motorcycle streaked down the driveway.

Matthew had only half-risen from his chair when the sound of Brian's bike faded completely. Sighing, he sat back down and studied his partially completed letter.

"Life's such a bitch sometimes," he murmured.

At length, he picked up his pen and started writing again. An hour later, he began to make more telephone calls.

Chapter Three

At forty-seven years old, Yeoh Chin Choo was finally the principal member of an aristocratic family whose successful business ventures had made its members wealthy for many generations. A full-bodied man with a squarish head and close-cropped hair, he paced in his office along a wall that was lined with aquariums containing extremely rare and lovely tropical fish.

Chin stopped to examine a particular two-inch-long specimen that sported electric blue and flaming orange fins that appeared to glow with a light of their own. A slow smile spread across his face. The fish was beginning to court a new female he had introduced into the tank the day before. These aquariums were his only distraction from the world of business.

"Is he here yet?" Chin barked in Mandarin Chinese at the intercom linking his private world with his outer office. Not waiting for an answer, he continued, "Show him in the moment he arrives." Yeoh Chin Choo was used to issuing orders.

The roomy glass-walled office was situated on the top floor of the eight-story Yellow Dragon Hotel, which he had recently opened in downtown Taipei, the capital city of the island of Taiwan. Mr. Yeoh had designed and directed the construction of this palatial temple of luxury with such great care and expense that he had felt a justifiable burst of pride when the premier travel magazine, *Destinations*, called it "a 5-star delight" in its review.

The Yellow Dragon was continuously filled by a steady stream of affluent travelers. Many were foreign officials drawn by government trade missions and businessmen from around the globe. At night this glittering hotel, with its various discos and bars, became the hot center for nightlife in this city of two and a half million people.

A moment later the intercom responded, "He's just coming in now, sir."

Matthew stepped through the doorway and stopped when he reached the rich Persian carpet. In his crossed hands, he held the handles of a small briefcase.

"Hello, Mr. Clark," Chin greeted him in perfect English. "Did you have a good flight into Taiwan?"

"Yes, thank you. This is quite a hotel you have here."

"Thank you. Please sit down. Would you care for a drink?"

"Thanks. Tea please... Chinese tea."

Chin looked flattered, and nodded to the servant who had quietly entered the room behind Matthew and who was now standing at attention near the door. The servant silently turned and left the room.

"I've reread your proposal, Mr. Clark, and I assume that you are convinced that it will succeed. Otherwise, you would not be here in Taipei... is this not so?" Yeoh Chin Choo had formally started the business meeting.

"Yes, I know there is a certain risk of failure in this venture but I think that my team and I can find and capture the Thylacine that I saw that night," Matthew replied, falling into the cadence of a business negotiation.

It had taken Matthew more than two months of hard work to locate and contact a potential buyer for his proposed product. A Thylacine captured alive would be a real one-of-a-kind item and it demanded a hefty fee.

"Do you have any particular questions that I may be able to answer?" Matthew asked.

"No, I think we've covered most of the basics through our correspondence. Ah... here's the tea."

The quiet servant brought in a silver tray and set it down on the large table that separated the two of them. Chin lifted the teapot, filling first one cup and then the other. Matthew chose a cup and placed it in front of himself.

Offering some small biscuits, Chin continued, "Tea is a valuable tradition that provides time to understand one's situation, don't you think so, Mr. Clark?"

"I've never looked at it quite that way, Mr. Yeoh, but it does give me time to look around. Say, isn't that a *Panchax* in breeding color over in that middle aquarium?"

"Ah!" exclaimed Chin, "you <u>know</u> this fish?"

"Well, somewhat," Matthew replied. "It's the only genus of vertebrate in the world whose eggs can stand total desiccation. They live on the African plains in the temporary pools left over from rainstorms. The pools may last only a few weeks before they dry and these fish must complete their life-cycle accordingly. When the puddle dries, the adult fish die, but their eggs can wait for years in the hard-baked mud for the next big rainstorm. I've only seen them once in the wild."

"Very good!" Chin was beginning to sound genuinely enthusiastic. "Come over and have a close look at them. See here... I raised these from eggs flown in from the Kalahari Desert. My agent there is a trained collector and he recently sent me a dried mud sample dug from over three metres below the surface of the ground. I had two soil scientists look at it and they both estimated the mud to be perhaps as much as two or three thousand years old."

"Incredibly, six fish hatched from the mud when we incubated it, though two failed to grow and have since died."

"I have studied this genus as thoroughly as possible, Mr. Clark, and I am certain that what you see in this - and that far tank over there - are the only swimming remnants of a lost species."

"Very impressive," Matthew commented with perfect honesty. "And very lovely, too."

Chin led the way back to the table.

"So, you see, Mr. Clark, your proposal intrigues me. I enjoy one-of-a-kind things and a captive Thylacine would bring people here from all over the world just to see it."

24

"I like you, Mr. Clark, but more importantly, I like to gamble on a potentially good investment... this is something that my family has excelled at for more than one hundred and fifty years."

"I will agree to your asking price of two million Australian dollars," Chin continued, "if you can deliver one of these animals to me alive."

"What if we catch two of them?"

"For a mated pair, I will give you five million dollars, Mr. Clark. Furthermore, since I've already had some of my people check you out and you are indeed probably the only man alive who can accomplish what you propose, I will advance you $180,000.00 to help you with your search.

Mind you, though... if the hunt is canceled or if you default on this agreement, I will have my 'collectors' contact you for repayment - with interest."

"And if I go through with the search and find nothing?" Matthew asked.

"If you search for more than six months and you find nothing, then - and only then - will I be willing to take a loss on my investment. Is this agreeable to you, Mr. Clark?"

Matthew hesitated, pouring himself another cup of tea. He had never dealt with such high stakes before. But if he did his job honestly and still failed, he had a way out.

"Okay," he agreed," but only if you allow us to transfer our catch to your custody in a neutral zone. It will be your responsibility to carry the 'product' to

Taiwan or wherever you wish."

"Agreed, Mr. Clark. I expect that we will have no problem bringing the animals into Taiwan though. You see, my country did not sign the CITES Treaty that regulates international trade in rare and endangered species. However, it is still a very good idea to remain discreet until we're ready to announce to the world what we have."

"Indeed," Matthew concurred.

"I'll have my secretary draw up our agreement while we have lunch, if you will," invited Chin respectfully. "Please come with me down to our restaurant; we have an excellent chef that I 'borrowed' from one of the best hotels in Singapore. While we eat, we can begin discussing some of the details of how we'll get your 'product' over here once you secure it."

Two days later, when Matthew's taxi arrived at the Taipei airport for the return trip to Hobart, he was confident that Chin's transportation preparations would be adequate if he actually caught a Tasmanian tiger. With luck, the transfer would be completed in less than twenty-four hours. The man from Taiwan would then have the world's only Thylacine and Matthew Clark would be a millionaire.

Chapter Four

In the golden light that follows sunrise, Michael Strezelecki carried the last bags containing his gear out to the helicopter and placed them on top of the huge pile of containers resting on the tarmac of the Deloraine Airport. Since the pilot was still in the office filing a flight-plan and Matthew was still driving the highway, there was little for Michael to do except to sit down on the largest and most sturdy-looking box and roll himself a cigarette.

Nicknamed "The Kid" by all those who knew him, he had called this morning the "most portentous day" of his life. At twenty-seven, he had grown up in Tasmania's mountainous interior tending his father's sheep. Physically tough and an expert tracker, he had become a true "bushy" who was only entirely comfortable while in a wilderness setting.

Until he was invited to join this expedition, his social life consisted mostly of hanging out in the nearest pub, drinking prodigious quantities of beer until he became obnoxious, and ending the evening in a fight or jail, or both. Today, however, Michael was sober and contented. He finally had a purpose and he was heading back into his beloved central highlands to fulfill it. Seven years ago he had seen a Thylacine himself but, until recently, he had never dared mention it to anyone.

The pilot had left his office and was walking

towards the helicopter just as Matthew's car came into sight at the far gate. They both arrived at the pile of equipment at the same time.

"G'day, mate," Matthew greeted the pilot. "She ready to fly?"

"One hundred percent!" the pilot answered.

"Good," Matthew continued. "Let me introduce the rest of the crew. Michael, here, grew up in the region near where we're going and is our best tracker."

Nods and handshakes all around.

"Victor Seigel, who I fetched last night from the international airport in Hobart, was originally a Yank. He has hunted and trapped nearly every kind of animal you can name."

More nods and handshakes.

"We left Hobart this morning around 2:00 AM in order to get here on time. Shall we get going?"

Willing hands began to stow gear in the helicopter's limited baggage space and then onto the rear passenger seat.

"The 'Kid' and I will go ahead, locate our base camp, and begin setting up," Matthew instructed. "The chopper will come back for you and the rest of the supplies... okay, Victor?"

Victor nodded his assent. The Bell Jet-Ranger helicopter could carry up to four passengers in a pinch, but it did not have enough room for everyone and all of the equipment still sitting on the pavement.

The three men climbed into the helicopter, Matthew in the copilot's seat, and Michael in back with his legs draped over a bag of provisions.

"See you in a while," Matthew called to the man on the ground, who closed the door and stepped back out of the way.

Fastening his seat-belt, Matthew looked back to make sure Michael had done the same and then turned his face expectantly towards the pilot. The pilot nodded, held his closed hand in the thumbs-up position, and started the engine.

After checking his gauges, he opened the throttle. The whining engine began to roar. In a few moments, they were high above the town of Deloraine and moving in a southwesterly direction towards the dark line of distant mountains called the Great Western Tier.

"Push this button on your intercom cable to talk. Let off to listen," instructed the pilot. "But please be quiet when I want to talk to the air traffic controller... anyway, we won't be needing him much where we're going."

The aircraft pulsed forward, bringing the mountainous shapes on the horizon nearer. Soon they were flying over a treetop canopy, broken only by open lakes and the rocky hills that pushed up through it.

An hour and a half had passed when the pilot announced, "We're getting close to the coordinates that you gave me, Matthew. How shall we proceed from here?"

"Follow Michael's advice," Matthew replied into the intercom.

They were near the spot where he had made camp the night he had seen the Thylacine. Hovering two hundred and fifty feet above the ground, they studied the landscape below.

"Recognize anything?" asked the pilot.

"It looks completely different from up here," Matthew replied.

"What do you think, Kid?"

"Let's fly up this valley for a while, okay?" Michael suggested, but he had forgotten to press the "talk" button on the intercom and his words were drowned by the engine noise.

"What was that?!"

"I said, let's fly up this valley for a while, okay?" This time he remembered to press the intercom button.

"The forest begins to open up further on and we might find a good spot to set the chopper down and make our camp," Michael explained. He was feeling useful and necessary. "See there, where those two streams come together, she's got a wide grassy spot that I think might be the place for us."

"Sounds good, Kid. Let's have a look."

The helicopter floated noisily up the valley.

"Nah!" said Michael in disgust when they had approached within a few hundred metres of the site. "Too many trees. Let's try that little adjoining valley over there."

Following Michael's pointing finger, the pilot turned the aircraft and slid it along the indicated path.

"There, Matthew, what do you think?"

"Looks good, Kid. Seems open enough... can you put down here?"

"No problem, mate," the pilot assured Matthew and began lowering his collective control in preparation for a landing.

The aircraft slowed to fifty knots, then thirty ... twenty ... ten ... until it hovered only five feet above the ground. Touchdown was so gentle that they hardly noticed the actual moment of contact.

As soon as the equipment was unloaded, the helicopter headed back towards Deloraine. Its return flight would be faster with the aircraft empty, but it would still have less than twenty-five or thirty minutes of fuel left upon arrival at the airport. This was a close flight that left little margin for delays.

"Let's start making camp, Kid!" said Matthew.

Two cabin tents were unrolled and erected near a small grove of white-barked eucalyptus trees. One packing box held six foldable chairs; another contained a surprisingly large folding camp table. By the time Victor arrived three hours later, the clearing was already beginning to look like "home."

After the helicopter was unloaded again and the pilot waved off, they erected two more tents in the expanding base camp. One was for Victor's use and the other was to function as a darkroom laboratory.

By sunset, the kitchen area was in operation with Victor serving as camp cook. The term "cook" was perhaps an underrating of Victor Seigel's consummate skill. He was more like a gourmet chef in this regard.

Actually, it would be safe to say that this man was extraordinary in everything he did.

Victor had grown up in central Manhattan but had broadened his horizons from that city's narrow canyons of concrete and glass at an early age. Even Central Park's gang-haunted nights became too parochial for him and he began to roam the world looking for adventure. Now, at forty something years old, Victor's experiences had mellowed him to the point where he called a soldier of fortune, "a seeker of cheap thrills." Exceptionally fit in body and spirit, he was still willing to overcome almost any hardship for a promised monetary reward.

...

The camp became active long before the bright disk of the new day's sun had erased the early spring chill of morning. Michael had already slipped away into the forest nearly two hours before first light.

Just after sunrise, a stray beam of tree-filtered orange-yellow light illuminated two men, Victor and Matthew, sitting next to an array of cameras and electronic equipment spread across the large table. Their breath steamed in the cold air. Each man held a hot cup of billy tea while before them sat two plates containing the scraps of a steak and egg breakfast.

"There's enough equipment here, Victor, to maintain eight camera stations," Matthew said. "Let's assemble them all now and make the necessary tests before we set any up in the bush. Hopefully, the 'Kid' will have found our first trial sites by this afternoon."

Between bites of food and sips of tea, they connected wires, loaded film, checked batteries, and tested motor drives. A noisy flock of Green rosellas landed above them in the camp's tallest eucalyptus tree, commenting with flute-like whistles upon the unfamiliar scene below. Smiling, Matthew stopped to look at the little parrots. This place was already beginning to feel like home to him; it was good to be back in the bush.

The work on the camera traps proceeded fairly smoothly; by noon, three of the units were ready for testing. First an infrared triggering unit was aligned with a reflector positioned several feet away. The invisible beam, pulsing several times a second, hit the reflector and was sent back to the sending unit. A receptor on that unit could detect if a moving object had interrupted the beam. If so, it would electronically close a switch that activated the camera.

Timed to the shutter were a pair of electronic flash units positioned six feet on either side of the camera. Aimed at the area where the camera's lens was pre-focused, they were held in position by mounting brackets screwed into nearby trees and shrubs.

Victor walked through the beam of the first trigger. The flash units responded instantly when the camera's shutter was released. Immediately, the "bzzzzt" sound of a camera-mounted motor-drive reset the unit for the next shot. Matthew gently tossed a stick into the infrared beam's path. Again both flashes winked and the motor drive labored into action.

"Looks good," Matthew commented approvingly. "Let's put in some film and check to make sure the housings are waterproof."

Each camera was loaded with a thirty-six exposure cassette of high-speed black and white film. After being placed in its plastic housing, it was dunked into a pail of water for a few moments to check for bubbles which would indicate a leak. One after another, all of the cameras and flash units were tested in the same manner.

Michael arrived back in camp around noon, just in time for lunch. As usual, Victor prepared a gourmet banquet from their rather ordinary supplies of camp vittles. While Matthew fussed with a stubborn PC plug on one of the camera housings, his two assistants discussed the possibilities of the "Big Reward."

"A half-million to a million dollars apiece, mate, just think of that!" remarked Michael. "Of course the 'boss' gets a larger share, but he's also been bankrolling this outfit."

"Yeah, a million would help me renew my life style," mused Victor, smiling. "But that's only if we catch two of these critters. If we go back empty-handed, we'll get no more than the advance that Matthew gave us."

"Victor... you still maintaining several addresses around the world?" Matthew queried.

"Got a place in Vancouver and that pad near Bondi Beach over in Sydney where you found me."

"You ever been married?" asked Michael.

34

"Nah! Can't be bothered..." Victor replied. "Anyway, I've got a steady girl at each place... sort of keeping house for me you might say. How about you, Kid?"

"Not me! At least not for a few more years anyhow," Michael replied while taking out tobacco and paper to roll a cigarette.

"All this running around must be wearing you down a bit, Victor," Matthew prodded. "You must be pushing forty by now."

"Hey! I'm forty-three years young and I've still got all my own hair. That's better than you can say for yerself old man."

Matthew's hairline had risen noticeably since Victor had last seen him.

"Touchy, touchy... must be all those sweet babes that's keeping you going," Matthew joked.

"Sorry to hear the news about your wife, Matt," Victor said with a concerned look on his face. "She didn't have an easy time did she?"

Matthew stared into the smoking cook-fire and said nothing. The pain of his loss welled up and for a few moments the camp became quiet in empathy.

I've missed you for so long, Laura... he thought.

"So... Kid, did you find any likely spots to put our cameras today?" Victor inquired, breaking the silence.

"Yep, I've got a few. I'll take you out there as soon as you're ready."

"Let's all go together on the first round,"

Matthew said, brightening. "We can set up and test the cameras, then - since each of us will know where they are - we can take turns servicing them. Okay?"

"Sounds like a plan," replied Victor.

"Incidentally, Kid, let's not smoke out where we'll be setting up the cameras. Our quarry might not like the smell of tobacco. We don't want to do anything that might scare him off, would we?" Matthew asked.

"Hey no worries, mate. I'm fair dinkum in the bush."

Chapter Five

The first spot that Michael chose was along a game trail near where it crossed a rocky divide through the hills about five kilometres east of camp. Large rock outcrops and boulders formed a natural funnel, guiding animal movement into a narrow area and through a "slot" between two forest-covered hills. Several nearby Waratah bushes were displaying stunning masses of scarlet blossoms.

"Good choice, Kid," Matthew said in praise. "Now let's see if we can get one of these cameras into position and operating properly."

It took more than three-quarters of an hour for the three of them to fix the camera, flash units, and infrared trigger into place. The beam of the trigger was installed to scan a path about a foot and a half above the ground.

"Hopefully, this will keep a lot of the smaller animals, such as Tasmanian devils and Bandicoots, from wasting our time and our film," Matthew explained. "Not much we can do about the larger wallabies, though."

After pre-focusing the camera on a target held halfway between the trigger unit and its reflector, the entire camera system was switched on, module by module. Ready lights on each component glowed softly. Michael then passed a stick through the infrared beam while Victor and Matthew watched the two flash units.

"Flash! Bzzzzt!" Everything seemed to be working perfectly.

"Okay! One down, two to go," Michael cheered. "Come on, I'll show you the next place."

Site number two was located only one and a quarter kilometres north of the first spot. However, it crossed through some extremely difficult terrain, including a small swampy area. After two hours of tramping and wading through muddy water, the team finally entered a forested glen that fronted a steep cliff.

"They's a game trail that runs along the base of that cliff," said Michael pointing. "I reckon you might find a good site for your camera over there."

Examining the area around the well-worn trail, Matthew located a suitable spot to set up the camera trap. Although they were becoming experienced in the operation, installing and presetting the equipment still took more than half an hour. It was getting to be late afternoon.

"You say you still have another site for us, Michael?" Matthew asked.

"Yes, I know it will be evening soon, but that place is only about three kilometres west of here... it's northeast of our camp but kinda on the way home. I think we can easily get back before it's completely dark." "Okay Kid, lead the way."

About a half a kilometre from where the second camera was installed, the terrain suddenly became much easier for travel. They began to make good time but it was still very near dusk when the men arrived at Michael's third location.

"What do you think, sir?" Michael asked sincerely.

"Well now, let's have a quick look around," Matthew answered, somewhat flattered at being called "sir." "We can probably finish up here before it gets completely dark. And I'm sure you two trackers can get us back to camp in time for tea, right?"

"Hey! No worries!" Michael exclaimed.

"I'm impressed with you, Kid. You certainly got around this morning," Victor commented.

After a complete inspection of the area, they finally decided that it probably wouldn't work well as a camera site after all. It was a brushy tract that had several well-used animal trails, but they branched too much to provide any one spot with good traffic potential.

"Let's call it a day and get some supper," Matthew suggested. "We've done pretty good for starters."

The evening was moonless and darkness was almost complete before the party reached camp. Although everyone carried an electric torch, no one had used his. A friendly competition had sprung up between Michael and Victor and they were trying to see how easily they could guide Matthew through the gloom. They were in excellent spirits by the time they reached camp, started a fire, and unboxed the ingredients for one of Victor's creations.

"As usual, that was a great feed, Victor," Matthew said after he had eaten his fill. "Do you work as a chef when you're not out runnin' around?"

Smiling, Victor nodded and accepted the compliment.

"Anyway... let's turn in soon. We've got plenty of work ahead," Matthew continued. "In fact, I'm retiring to my tent now. See you at five-o'clock tomorrow."

He rose from the big table and picked his way to his tent without the aid of a torch-light.

"Good practice for me," he said to himself.

Once inside, he lit a gas lantern and sat on his cot to write up his diary. He could hear the friendly murmur of Michael and Victor chatting while they finished a mug of billy tea.

Seen from outside, Matthew's tent glowed translucently against the dark forest. The men at the table could see his silhouetted figure cast off his shirt and reach up to extinguish the light. Matthew's last conscious thought that night was how glad he was that the other two men got along so well together. He felt that he had put together a good team.

...

At 4:50 A.M., the smell of cooking breakfast sausages greeted Matthew as he stumbled out of his tent. It was still very dark.

"G'day! Mates," Matthew said brightly in greeting to his expedition teammates already seated under the glow of a lantern hanging above the table.

"G'day," they replied in chorus.

"Coffee ready?" Matthew asked.

"No worries, sir!" Michael responded. "Victor saved you a bit. We're already on our second mug."

Matthew chose a tin cup that didn't appear too dirty and offered it out to be filled. Victor willingly obliged and also handed him a plate of ham and eggs.

"Here's my plan for today, guys," Matthew began, trying to sound like a construction boss through a mouthful of food. "We've got two cameras out and we've got six more to set up."

"By now, each of us should be able set up one of these things by ourselves... so, we'll carry two of them in each of our packs when we branch out to look for new sites."

"Michael, why don't you head north towards the Walls of Jerusalem? That's the area where you spent a lot of time while you were growing up, isn't it?"

"Yes-sir," the "Kid" replied. "Hundreds of nice lakes in there."

"Okay," Matthew continued, "Victor will head east towards the Great Pine Tier and I'll go southwest for a look. If either of you discover a really good site for a camera, then go ahead and set it up. There's no hurry, though, we've got heaps of ground to explore. We'll meet back here at base camp tonight and see how we've done. Any questions?"

There were none.

"Let's get crackin' then," replied Victor as he

picked up two of the bundled camera kits and gently placed them into his pack. "See ya later, Kid."

Michael left immediately and soon vanished into the forest. Victor went about fifteen minutes later, after he had tidied up the kitchen area and packed himself some food. Not having as keen a night vision as the other two men, Matthew lingered over a second and then a third cup of coffee until dawn began to streak the dark clouds.

After packing a lunch and padding his cameras with some rain gear, Matthew set out in a south-westerly direction along a brush-filled gully that twisted and turned and finally ended in a rock outcrop that blocked the "saddle" of land connecting two small mountain peaks. Once he had crossed the saddle, he entered into another watershed that drained to the southeast.

"This must be the headwaters of the Nive River," he thought to himself. Following a stream upwards, he soon came to a small alpine-like lake. Here he discovered another good camera site.

The outlet of the lake flowed over a low sill of solid rock, creating a little falls about three feet high. Below the falls was an expanse of broken rubble bounded by sheer rock cliffs about twenty feet tall on either side of the stream. Any animal moving up from the lower drainage area to the lake would most likely pass through this chute.

A well-worn game trail along the creek indicated that Matthew was probably right in his estimation of the site. Squatting next to the trail, he slowly surveyed his surroundings, trying to imagine the best place to set up a camera that would intercept a Thylacine... perhaps one that was hurrying back to its den following a long night of hunting. After several minutes of squinting in various directions, he began to visualize the setup.

"The camera should go over there on that small tree. One of the flash units can be taped to that rock and the other could go in that bush..."

Action soon followed his mental blueprint and within a half an hour, the setup was in place, working perfectly. Packing up his remaining gear, he hiked around the little falls and out onto the shore of the lake. This bright body of water surrounded with stunted alpine trees presented such a charming scene that it reminded him of one those glowing landscape paintings by Australian aborigine artist Albert Namatjira.

About halfway along its eastern shore, he found the perfect place to stop for lunch. A broken boulder had split into two unequal halves about ten feet from the water's edge. Both pieces lay with flat side up, one about two feet above the other, like a bench and a table. In a nearby Scoparia bush that was smothered in yellow pea-like blossoms, a solitary Wattlebird hopped from branch to branch picking at insects attracted to the flowers' sweet scent. As Matthew sat and ate, he noticed that the fleshy wattles on the bird's neck were precisely the same color as the flowers.

Beneath his feet all around him, the rocks were

greened and softened by numerous growths of cushion plants. Putting out thousands of moss-like branchlets which formed a dense mat, these emerald colonies were spiced with a liberal sprinkling of other small plants, such as the tiny carnivorous sundews that had co-evolved within the cushions since the last glacial period, beginning about twenty-three thousand years ago.

Tasmania had once been linked to the Australian mainland by a land bridge over which plants and animals migrated. As the sea level became raised by glacial melt, Tasmania was cut off and life here on this island developed forms unlike those anywhere else on earth.

...

When the light of day found Michael, he was already several miles from camp. Alone, he moved instinctively and unhurried through the brush and rocky hills. His footsteps were quick and sure while his senses seemed to include everything around him... a wallaby scuttling into the undergrowth... a small gray owl resembling a patch of lichen on a sheltered branch... two carnivorous beetles attempting to claim the same tiny corpse of a diminutive bird. At this moment, Michael felt more at home than he had in over three years.

First, his father had died and then two years later, his elder brothers sold the homestead and all of its sheep in order to "take care of Mother." They had said

44

that it "was for the best" when they moved her to Devonport on the north shore of the Island. They had told him that Helen, his oldest brother's wife, would look after her.

That's what they said... but she didn't last more than six months. Her constant wish was to see the farm, to go home, but his brothers and Helen had said, "Now, now, Mum, it will be all right. We'll take you there in the spring, we promise." But by then it was too late.

After her death, Michael had gone back to the old homestead. The place had been purchased by a big hydro-development scheme and it sat empty and abandoned, waiting for the rising water from a new dam to flood over it. With tears streaming down his face, Michael had set fire to the old house and watched it burn to the ground before turning to leave. Since that day, most of his memories were a mad blur of fights and drunken nights... until now.

Michael stopped suddenly, sat on a fallen log and placed his hands to his face. Unexpected tears welled forth. When he stood up a few minutes later, he felt strangely refreshed and renewed.

...

By eleven o'clock, he had reached the southern "gate" to the Walls of Jerusalem, a unique geological region known mostly only to locals. Its huge natural amphitheater, more than thirty kilometres in diameter, contained over four hundred glacier-gouged lakes

45

surrounded by stony cliffs nearly three hundred and fifty metres high. There were only four "gates" or entrances into this world, three in the north and a stream-eroded gap in the southern rampart where he stood, surveying the open expanse before him.

This hidden realm was Michael's favorite place in the world. As a child, he had first heard about it from a few trappers and other "bushys," but had only discovered it for himself while out on a three-week-long bush trek from the homestead when he was seventeen. His father, a second generation settler, had also found the "gate" many years before, and the two had talked about going there together some day. Unfortunately, that day never came; the duties of the farm kept his father busy until death relieved him of his responsibility. Michael, however, continued to return to the "gate" at every opportunity until the homestead was abandoned.

This was also the place where he had seen the Thylacine and he quickly located a site in the gap where he could set up a camera station. Having completed the task, he then explored two of the nearest lakes before heading back to base camp.

...

For Victor, the eastern route became increasingly difficult with every step closer to the Great Pine Tier. The broken slopes of this line of craggy peaks were cloaked with a nearly impassable veneer of gnarled beeches and dwarf myrtles. Above them, here and there, rose the magnificent white trunks of ancient

46

Pencil pines. This antediluvian species can take up to fourteen hundred years to reach maturity.

A powerful climber, Victor finally cleared the tree-line and was immediately rewarded with an uninterrupted view back towards the west. From a rock promontory that jutted out from the ridge, he rested and surveyed the temperate rainforest-filled valley below.

Two crow-like Currawongs soared from a nearby rock perch and landed noisily in a tree beneath him. Although he had set up both of his cameras earlier, he noticed another likely spot a bit lower where a trail wound through some boulders. The Currawongs flew to the trail and began picking red berries from a bush. It was already four in the afternoon and Victor knew he would be late getting back to camp.

Still he lingered, feasting his eyes on the expansive scene and trying to imagine where he would be if he were a Thylacine. Victor was expert at second-guessing his quarry, as his many kills in Africa and India attested. When he was young, after he had left New York, he spent two years in the Sawtooth Wilderness of Idaho, trapping beavers, mink, and Mountain lions. The lions were extremely difficult to catch and presented Victor with a challenge that he eagerly rose to pursue. He called that period of his life his "pure" days.

Uncomfortably, he thought of his years as a soldier-for-hire and all the killing that had involved him. His career seemed splendid in those days, but no longer. The glory had faded completely in his mind, but the only time that he felt regrets was during moments like this - when the world seemed to lay at his feet.

...

Darkness was complete when Victor returned to camp that night. Only Michael, with his ears tuned to local sounds, knew that Victor had waited for a while just outside of camp, listening.

"Hi-ho! Mate, did you lose something beyond the camp?" Michael jokingly greeted him. Victor was surprised that Michael had heard his stealthy return.

"Naw, I thought I saw a snake," he replied. "How ya doin', Kid?

Both men laughed. No one was kidding anyone.

"How'dja do?" Matthew inquired.

"I put both cameras out and made it to the flanks of the Tier," answered Victor.

"Good on ya, mate! Michael set up one camera and I put up both of mine: one on the way out and other on the way back," Matthew reported. "Care for a cupper?"

Taking the proffered cup of tea, Victor eased himself onto one of the benches surrounding the table. The three men talked about the day's experiences until the gas lantern suddenly sputtered and went out.

For a few moments they were quiet until Matthew laughed, "I guess I forgot to check the fuel level before lighting it. Hold a spotlight on it, will you Kid?"

"We'll check each camera every seven days," Matthew continued, changing the subject as he refilled the lantern with fuel. "That way they'll have enough time to lose our scent and become part of the scenery. The batteries are good for a fortnight before they have to be recharged."

"I've got spares here plus heaps of new film if we need it. The used batteries can be charged with a little solar panel that I brought along. We'll just rotate them as they get depleted."

"Victor, would you like to go with Michael tomorrow to find a spot for the last camera?"

"Sure!" responded Victor. "Whadda you say we go out to a place that I spotted over at the 'Tier'? Feel like gettin' out-hiked, Kid?"

"Hah! That will be the day," Michael retorted, answering the challenge.

"Great! Be sure to keep your eyes out for extra camera locations; we probably should move our stations around a bit until we get some action," Matthew added.

"I'll stay in camp tomorrow to tidy up my notes and ready some more of the equipment. Oh, yes, I promise to have supper fixed by the time it gets dark. It won't be as good as your cooking, Victor, but it should fill the gap."

Chapter Six

Victor and Michael quietly left camp before daybreak, allowing Matthew to sleep late. Both men were expert trackers and, like some Aborigines, seemed to be able to "see" in the dark. Until they met on this expedition, however, neither man had ever known anyone else who displayed "bush" talent equal to theirs. Victor had the wider experience but this was Michael's home ground.

The friendly competition that sprang up between them spurred each man to do his best and perhaps even a little better than he had before. It was a way of testing your skills against someone who could appreciate them.

They reached the slope of the "Tier" at one o'clock in the afternoon. After the camera was set up and tested, they traveled for a stretch along the flanks of the "Tier" towards the southern "gate." Just before they headed back to camp, Michael told Victor about "his" place. Following a short discussion, they agreed to return to base camp and let Matthew know that they wished to hike to the Walls of Jerusalem area together. They had a few free days before any of the camera stations needed checking. On the return trip, they planned to pass through camp again for new supplies before going back out to the "Tier" to check Victor's setups.

"I reckon you'll like the place when you see it,"

said Michael happily. He was feeling carefree again - and a little like Victor's son - and he enjoyed it. He had missed his own father for a long time. Now he had a friend that he could share his favorite places with.

When Michael and Victor neared base camp, they decided to have a bit of fun. While Matthew fussed with a boiling pot, the two men attempted to sneak along the ground to the table, sit down at it, and pick up a cup as if they were drinking tea... before they were discovered. Both Victor and Michael made it to the table and got seated all right, but Michael accidentally bumped a tin plate and caused it to crash to the ground.

"What the...? Well! How ya going?" Matthew exclaimed in surprise. "Playing tricks on me, eh?"

There was a great deal of laughter that evening as they downed a hearty meal of camp bread and stew. All the cameras were now set up and there was time to relax.

The next morning was overcast by leaden clouds and chilled by a penetrating south wind that seemed to come directly from Antarctica. Victor and Michael were busy packing their gear for the trip through the "gate" and into the Walls of Jerusalem area. Matthew agreed that this trip would be useful to the expedition, for few people had explored that southern section, but he voiced caution: there could be snow up there in two or three days.

"It's still Spring, ya know, and the weather can do just about anything it wants to with little warning,"

Matthew cautioned. "I've got a little handheld VHF radio that you can take with you if you like.

I've raised an aerial and gotten the big base unit in my tent working. Yesterday, while you guys were out, I even managed to contact Sam Strickland, our chopper pilot, during a frequency test.

The little radio only transmits about five watts of power, so its range is limited to just a few miles unless you are up on a open ridge or something," Matthew continued. "However, our base unit has a good aerial and has over forty watts of transmitting power. If you're in the clear, I'll probably be able to talk to you."

"Okay, Matthew, I'll carry your handheld, but we probably won't be needing it... that is unless we see a Thylacine," said Victor smiling.

"I'll listen for your call between 6:00 and 6:15 every evening on Channel forty-two," Matthew said. "I hope to do some exploring of the local terrain myself but I'll make a point of being back in camp by 5:30... so let's give 'er a test tonight and see if she works, okay? Use the tag 'Mobile One' to I.D. yourself. The base unit is licensed as 'Bio-Camp.'"

"One more thing," he added. "Keep your transmissions short in order to conserve battery power."

"Thanks, Matthew, we'll give you a shout tonight by radio," Victor said as he shouldered his pack.

"See ya later, sir," Michael sang cheerfully as they tramped out of camp.

Victor and Michael reached the "gate" and the

53

site of the first camera before noon. Not wishing to disturb the site, they carefully circumvented the camera by climbing part way up the wall and traveling along a narrow bench in the rock. The shelf eventually petered out in a scree of broken rock and the men boulder-hopped their way back down to the valley floor. The air temperature was markedly cooler here.

"This is it, Victor!" Michael exclaimed as they entered the "gate." "See how that huge cliff encircles this valley?"

"Wow! This really is like a lost world," agreed Victor.

The cloud-darkened sky seemed to melt into the tops of the cliff creating the illusion that it did not end but simply faded from sight above the viewer. Up high, an erratic breeze sent wraiths of broken clouds spilling and tumbling over the cliff's rocky brim and into the basin.

"Matt was right, we might get a bit of snow tonight," observed Michael. "If we do, we can look for Thylacine footprints in the morning. Come on I'll show you where I once saw one several years ago. I've never mentioned it to anyone, except you and Matthew."

For the rest of the day, the two men circled clear lakes and traversed small creeks as they moved into the interior of the big basin. Sometimes they would travel on opposite shores of a lake until they met again at its far end. This gave them a good opportunity to look for signs of wildlife and animal traffic patterns.

By 5:00 PM, the heavy sky seemed to have

lowered until it was just touching the tops of the tallest trees. A light drizzle of rain began to fall.

"Hey Kid, let's make camp beneath that over-hanging boulder over there," Victor suggested. "I'll whip up some grub. You hungry?"

"Sounds good, mate," Michael acknowledged. "I'll set up the alpine camp stove." This stove ran on petrol and cooked very efficiently. It also did not emit smoke or leave a telltale campfire trace of half-burnt charcoal.

"It's funny how many blokes insist on having a huge roaring camp fire when they're out in the bush," Michael observed. "When I have a fire, it's always quite small, kind of personal like. You know what I mean, Victor?"

Victor agreed. There was no sense in burning valuable wood and sending up lots of smoke and flames. It would be a dead giveaway of your position, plus it's a lot of work to maintain. A good cooking fire should be only about eight or nine inches in diameter and give off no smoke at all.

It was soon time for the radio call to Matthew. Victor climbed a large mound of glacial till located a couple of hundred metres away.

"Bio-Camp, Bio-Camp, this is Mobile One. Over."

Victor waited for about a minute for a response and then he repeated the message. "Bio-Camp, Bio-Camp, this is Mobile One. Over."

"Mobile One, this is Bio-Camp," came a strong

reply from the radio's speaker. "How you going, Victor? Over."

"Just fine, Matthew, we're expecting snow tonight from the looks of things. Over."

"I'm getting some rain down here," Matthew noted. "Hopefully it won't last too long. Over."

"We had a good day of hiking but didn't see anything special," reported Victor. "How'd you do?"

"Same, same... but then we're just getting started," Matthew said. "Right?"

"Yeah! NO WORRIES, MATE," Victor said in a mock Australian accent. "Talk to you tomorrow, Matt. Over."

"Right! This is Bio-Camp out."

The overhanging rock proved to be a good shelter because it began to snow about an hour and a half before dawn. By daylight, five or six centimetres of snow had already blanketed the rocky valley. It was still snowing heavily when Victor and Michael finished their breakfast and started on their second cup of tea.

"No use in wandering about in this stuff," Victor commented. "All the animals, including our Thylacines, are going to stay put until it stops snowing."

With their legs wrapped in their sleeping bags and their backs propped up by the sheltering rock, the two men talked about bush-craft and reminiscenced while the snow fell silently all around them. The overhang formed a lee where snow could not collect; so the campsite was the only patch of bare ground in sight.

By noon, and several more cups of tea, thirteen

centimetres of snow had accumulated. The blizzard began to slacken off by early afternoon and stopped completely by 4:00 PM. A faint sun attempted to make its appearance through the clouds and mist, an indication that the weather was trying to clear. The men decided to go and look for animal tracks after the evening meal.

"See these long tracks with the little bitty marks on either side of them?" asked Michael. "These are the footprints of a wallaby. A potoroo track looks much the same, just smaller.

"Hmmmm," Victor replied. He had no qualms about learning from someone much younger than him. After all, this was his first trip into the wilderness of Tasmania.

"Here, Victor, those are the tracks of a Tasmanian devil. I call these critters 'land sharks.' They'll eat practically anything... even chew up the bones, so there's not even a scrap left behind. It's said that a devil can eat a third of its own weight in about an hour."

"Holy mackerel! That's like eating fifty hamburgers in one sitting," Victor exclaimed.

"One of these devils will probably get me when I die," Michael avowed. "Won't be nothing left of me 'cept my belt buckle."

Both men chuckled at this mental image and continued their search for tracks in the telling snow.

"What's this? They look like hoof prints!" asked Victor in surprise. "I'd say that they were made by a deer."

"They <u>were</u> made by a deer," Michael replied.

"I didn't realize there were deer here in Tasmania. They're not native are they?"

"They're Fallow deer from Europe. I was told that they were introduced back in 1939 by the local hunting clubs. They're all over the interior now. Good eatin', too."

Darkness began to overtake the pair as they rounded the southern bay of a tree-rimmed lake. The trees' short gnarly branches starkly contrasted with the white background and were repeated by reflection in the lake's dark waters. New snowflakes began to fall, kissing the water's surface.

"More snow tonight," Michael stated as he watched the snow particles vanish into the black water.

"Let's go back to our 'lodging,' have some supper, and make ourselves comfortable," suggested Victor humorously.

At six o'clock that evening, Michael tried his hand at using the radio.

"This is Bio-Camp," Matthew responded when he received the hail. "That you, Kid?"

"Yes-sir!" said Michael, pleased with himself. "I just thought I might give this thing a try, too," he added somewhat humbly. "Er, over!"

"How was the snowfall up there? Over."

"Not bad, sir, about thirteen centimetres. Looks like we'll be getting a bit more tonight. Over."

"Well, keep warm, Kid. Over."

"Yes-sir. We'll do that."
"This is Bio-Camp out."

Chapter Seven

Five more centimetres of snow fell around them that night. Just after dawn, they broke camp and headed towards the western "wall." Although travel was hampered somewhat by the deeper snow, it also had cleaned the wilderness slate to record new animal activity. The searching men found plenty of signs of bird and animal movement in the area, but not even so much as a hint of a Thylacine. They began to talk about widening the search into new areas.

"I know of a secret way up the western wall," Michael revealed. "If we travel a half-dozen kilometres north along its base, we'll come to a small creek that spills over the top edge and tumbles down in a series of drops. It's a bit of climb and this snow doesn't help much, but I reckon we can do it all right."

"Once we are up on top, we can swing around towards the southwest and return to the 'gate' from outside. Then we can check out the camera while we're there. What do you say, Victor?"

"Okay, Kid, lead the way. It doesn't look like this snow is going to last for very long, anyway. Look, it's already beginning to melt off the bushes."

As the men worked their way along the bottom of the "wall," the sun came out and the air became noticeably warmer. Soon they could see a large black streak where the falling stream had washed the snow from the rocky cliff.

The first leg of the climb went fairly easily but the second rise was much more difficult. The smooth rock offered few places for a secure handhold or purchase with a booted foot.

"The old stream's cut a deep a notch in the wall, Victor. We'll have to do a bit of chimneying but we'll be laughing once we reach that flare at the top. Stay close to me, or you'll be getting wet from the spray," instructed Michael.

With Michael leading the way, the two men began inching their way up the steep rocky slope. Over the centuries, the falling stream had eaten a series of stepped gullies in the cliff's face. When the men finally reached the second bench, the hardest part of the climb was over. Exhausted, they sat and gazed out over the lake-studded valley below them.

"I can see why you claim this area as your 'own,'" Victor conceded. "Even covered in snow, it's special."

Far above the resting men, an old gum tree log lay angled on the slope. Long ago, one end of it had been jammed against a boulder by the force of its fall. Its other end reclined against a loose pile of broken rock and branches. For many years it had rested firmly in this position. Small animals frequently used it as a convenient "runway" to the other side of the gully where the slope was less steep. But the branches that helped hold this matrix of loose rubble together were rotten. A small limb had broken under the weight of this morning's snow, causing the pile to shift ever-so-slightly, changing the equilibrium of the log and rocks that had lain together for so long.

As he crossed over the gully for the final leg of his climb, Michael momentarily leaned his weight onto the uphill side of the log. The old trunk had looked stable but it instantly gave way, trapping Michael's feet in the roll of rocks beneath it.

Instinctively, he fell onto his back and tried to kick himself free of the rock-slide but the sweep of the falling log caused more rocks to begin tumbling down the chute. Unable to stop himself from skidding down the slope, Michael did manage to push himself away from the trunk, which crashed and tumbled in front of him.

The drop had started to become exceedingly steep when Michael slid into a small tree, slowing his descent. His flying weight broke several branches, lacerating his arm as he passed over them. Making a desperate grab, he managed to hold on for a few moments. Those precious seconds slowed his downward momentum and allowed the log and most of the rock-slide to drop over the precipice below him.

Then the limb broke and Michael began skidding again towards empty space. As he gathered momentum, he frantically searched for anything that might stop his plunge to certain death. Below and a metre to the right of him was a small knob of rock protruding from the precipitous slope. This was Michael's only chance and he had less than two seconds in which to take it. As he slid down the rock face, he

63

rolled towards where the protrusion would soon be. Sliding now on his side, he grabbed at it with locked elbows, as it came rushing up toward him.

The force of impact nearly knocked him unconscious but somehow he held on. His backpack split open, its contents clattered down the rock face, then hurdled silently into space. Part of the pack's frame stabbed into his shoulder but there was nothing he could do but simply hold on.

"Victor!" Michael called.

Victor was several feet behind Michael when the accident occurred and had quickly braced himself when the slide began. Peering cautiously down the sharp slope, he could not see Michael, though he could hear his cries. Michael had stopped below a shoulder in the rock face and was hidden from view.

"Can you hear me?" Victor called.

"Yes!"

"Are you all right?"

"No! I'm hung up on a rock.. I won't be able to hang on very long!"

Victor needed to move quickly.

"I've got some rope, I'll try and get it down to you, Kid!" he called.

"I can't let go to grab it!" Michael cried.

Victor searched for a way down, towards the sound of Michael's voice, but there weren't any footholds. Somehow, he would have to lower himself on the rope, but first he needed to secure it.

The nylon line was forty metres long and

although its diameter was significantly smaller than an ordinary climbing rope, it was quite strong. It could be wrapped up into a small bundle and Victor found it useful enough to always include it in his field pack. However, he did not usually carry climbing hardware such as pitons or a hammer.

The only possible place for him to fix the rope seemed to be in a long, constricted, vertical crack in the rock face. Tying a large knot in the end of the rope, he shoved it into the crack. Pulling down on the rope, he jammed the knot into its narrowest part.

After jerking on the rope several times to make sure the knot had seated itself, Victor leaned into the rope to test his weight. The rope seemed secure and he cautiously began abseiling down the arduous slope.

"I certainly hope that knot holds," he whispered under his breath.

Michael was beginning to drift in and out of consciousness from the enormous effort it took to cling to the rocky protrusion. His locked arms seemed to scream with pain, but he continued to hold on. After a seeming eternity, Victor finally appeared above him amid a shower of loose stones.

"Sorry about that, Kid! You okay?" Victor called down to him. One rock about the size of a hen's egg had hit Michael in the head with a glancing blow, and it momentarily stunned him, almost causing him to lose his grip on the rock. Something warm and red began dripping into his left eye, clouding his vision.

He tried to call out to Victor but didn't have

enough energy to do so. All of his strength was now being focused into just hanging on. Little by little, he could feel his grip beginning to fail. He knew that when the moment came, it would happen all at once; his hold would slip and he would slide out into space. All that remained of his consciousness was his burning will to survive. He was unaware of the renewed shower of rocks that rained down from above.

"Well now, let's see what we can do to get you attached to this rope," said Victor when he had finally worked his way down to Michael's grim figure. "Can you hear me, Kid?"

Michael was too weak to answer; it was all he could do to lift his head to look at him. Victor had to work fast. He began threading the loose end of the rope around Michael's chest beneath his arms.

"Hang on, Kid. Just a little longer. Just a little longer. There... I've got this thing around you. Now, I'll just tie a loop knot and we'll be set. Don't give up!"

Michael had already begun to slip when a strong hand grabbed his arm and stopped his downward movement.

"I can't hold the two of us for more than a few seconds," Victor said. "Get a new grip on that rock and I'll go back up some place where I can plant my feet and pull you up."

Michael's eyes rolled wearily and his head nodded slightly in acknowledgment.

"This rope is not well secured and I'm not sure it will hold the two of us. Don't put any weight on it until

I give you the word," Victor cautioned him. "Okay, I'm going back up!"

Using the rope to steady himself, Victor half-walked, half-climbed his way back to a spot just below where the knot had been jammed into the crack. Here, a small rocky shelf offered a place to sit and brace against Michael's weight.

"Okay, Kid, let's get you out of there!" called Victor after he had tightened the slack in the rope by pulling it around his waist. "Come on up!"

Michael let go of the rock and felt his arms fall to his sides. His body slid a few inches downward and then stopped. Victor's rope was holding him.

"I can't pull you up without your help!" Victor shouted. "But I _can_ hold you while you get some strength back."

Michael lay upon the rock face with his eyes closed and tried to push back his weariness. Breathing deeply, he began to surface towards the new task at hand. The rope pinched his backpack and cut the circulation under his arms. But his hands were free and they began to move from the power of renewed will. His first attempt at crawling up the steep slope ended in collapse. He had moved, however, nearly two feet above the rocky protrusion.

"Take your time, Kid!" Victor shouted in encouragement. "I can hold you."

Breathing heavily, Michael lay upon the rock face and rebuilt some of his strength. Finally, he grabbed the rope above him with both hands and pulled himself up into a half-crouch. With a laborious duck-like waddle, he worked his way up over the rock shoulder and back to where Victor could see him.

To keep the line's tension on Michael, Victor pulled tight each slackened foot of rope that passed around his waist. Every time Michael stumbled and fell, Victor simply hung on and waited for him to recover his feet.

"Try and stand up, son. If you lean out from the slope, you'll find that you will have better stability," he hollered. "That's good... that's good. All right!"

When Michael finally reached the narrow shelf, he slumped down beside Victor.

"Thanks Victor, I thought I was a goner. I'm sure glad you carry that rope in your pack."

Michael's teeth began to chatter as he involuntarily shivered from exhaustion.

"Here, Michael, let's put some extra clothing on you to help keep you warm," Victor suggested. "And let's have a look at that injured arm."

Cutting away part of the bloodied jacket and shirt, Victor exposed the wounds in Michael's arm. There were three gashes in the large muscle of his forearm, the worst nearly ten centimetres long and bleeding profusely. Fortunately, no major arteries seemed to be involved. Victor removed his first-aid kit from his pack and opened it.

"We've got to stop that bleeding," he said as he applied a compress bandage. "After you've recuperated a bit, I'll help you climb the rest of the way out of here and we'll make camp up on top."

"I think a good blazing campfire would be in order too!" he added.

While Michael rested, Victor removed the rope's knotted end from the cracked rock. Not only had it held firmly throughout the ordeal, it actually required quite a bit of prying to release it.

"How you doing, Kid?" asked Victor when had he finished gathering the rope and returned to his side. "Think you'll be able to make it up to the top before it gets dark?"

Michael nodded and mumbled, "I reckon so."

Removing Michael's empty pack, Victor helped him make the slow climb. Above the gully, the slope became less steep, eventually becoming nearly flat for a thirty metres or so near the crest. The snow had been melting most of the day and large bare patches of rock showed through where the sun had warmed them.

"Let's make camp over here near these trees, Kid," suggested Victor. "First, we'll get you wrapped up snugly and then I'll get a fire and some coffee going. It might also be a good idea to put your arm in a sling for a while."

"When you're settled in, I'll go back for what's left of your gear."

The heat from the fire felt luxurious to Michael as he recovered from the shock of his injuries. The wound above his left eye had swollen, nearly closing off his vision. His head pounded and flickers of pain periodically racked him. But he was still alive and able to walk. The hot coffee really seemed to help.

When Victor returned with the remains of Michael's gear, he rebuilt the fire and then scouted around for a good supply of wood... enough to last through the night.

"Your sleeping gear went over the edge along with most of the rest of your things," Victor reported. "You can use my stuff until we get back... I'll be okay."

"Thanks, mate," said Michael gratefully.

At 6:00 PM, Victor brought out the little handheld VHF radio.

"Best give Matthew a call and let him know what's happened," he said. "Bio-Camp, Bio-Camp, this is Mobile One. Over."

No response. After waiting a minute, the call was repeated.

"Bio-Camp, this is Mobile One. Over."

"This is Bio-Camp," Matthew replied. "Your signal is weak and breaking up. Over."

Victor looked at the battery gauge on the top of the radio. It indicated, "Low". The radio had been on when he took it out to use it. Either it had been left on since its last use or it had been accidentally bumped to the "on" position during the crisis.

"Matt, we've had a bit of trouble. Michael's taken a bad spill, so we're going to be a bit slow coming out. Over."

"What was that?" Matthew asked.

"Trouble, we've had some trouble," Victor shouted. He knew the battery was about to fail.

"Trouble? What kind of trouble?" Matthew asked again, his concern rising. Only static filled the receiver.

Victor knew that he would not have enough battery power to transmit again, so he just listened to Matthew's broken questions until static completely overcame his reception.

"We're on our own, Kid," he told Michael. "Let's get as much sleep as we can."

Victor put on his remaining warm clothes and banked up the fire against a pile of rocks that would act as a heat reflector. Michael was already asleep.

Every few hours, Victor woke to add more wood to the fire. The night had begun to seem extraordinarily drawn-out to him by the time the first light of dawn began to brighten the sky. Fortunately, Michael had slept through it all.

In order to let Michael sleep as long as possible, Victor started breakfast without first waking him. However, in a few minutes, Michael woke up anyway.

"That coffee sure smells good, mate," he commented as he stretched stiffly.

"Sure does! Want a cup?" replied Victor as he filled a mug without waiting for an answer. "Here."

Michael sat up, taking the cup with his free hand.   "Well, Kid, think you can do any walking today?"

"I'll give 'er a go," Michael answered without conviction.

"Okay, but there's no hurry, you know," Victor

71

cautioned.

After they had broken camp, the two men worked their way very slowly towards the southwest, where the terrain was not quite so rough. After many rest stops, they reached the stream that flowed out of the southern "gate."

"Let's camp here, Kid," Victor said. "When you're nice and comfortable, I'll go up and check the camera."

"Go on ahead! I can take care of myself," said Michael stubbornly. He was beginning to feel like he would survive this ordeal after all.

The camera's frame-counter indicated that ten frames of film had been exposed. After rewinding the film and installing a new cassette, Victor replaced the camera in its waterproof housing. Then he checked the battery packs for the flash units.

After refocusing the lens, he passed his hand through the trigger beam to test the system. The flash units blinked and the camera whirred. Everything was in order. It was time to get back and see how Michael was getting along.

"Hey, mate!" Michael cheerily greeted him when he returned. "I've got some billy tea and fresh damper bread cooked up. You want to try some?"

"Sounds great, Kid. I didn't know that you were a chef too," he said in jest. Victor was relieved to see that the "Kid" was recovering some of his composure.

Chapter Eight

When Michael and Victor arrived in base camp, Matthew became very concerned about the lacerations in Michael's arm.

"Perhaps I should call in the chopper to take you out to a hospital," he suggested after inspecting Michael's injuries. One of the lacerations was more than a centimetre and a half deep. It had just missed a good-sized artery.

"No, please no! Just let me rest for a couple of days and I'll be good as new," Michael pleaded. The idea of leaving the expedition and his new friends was more than he cared to consider. "Victor said he'd sew a couple of stitches in me, if necessary."

"Well, nothing seems broken. I guess we can put up with you around here for a while," Matthew said, smiling. "If you feel like operating on him, Victor, he's all yours... However, if even the slightest infection sets in, you go to hospital. Okay?"

...

During the days that followed, Victor and Matthew examined every camera station that they had operating and removed and replaced any film that had been exposed in their absence. One camera's frame counter was reading "20" when they arrived to check it. Two others, however, had recorded no movement in more than a week. They would be moved to new locations if nothing had happened by the time they were visited again.

Back in camp, Michael tried to make himself useful as a one-handed cook's assistant, slowly washing dishes and stocking up wood for the cooking fire. He proved himself to be more valuable, however, as a photo-processing assistant.

In the darkroom tent, Michael and Matthew would wind the film of each cassette onto a plastic developing reel. Up to four reels were then placed into a canister filled with developer fluid. The canister was then sealed with a watertight lid and agitated every few seconds for a prescribed amount of time. After development, the lid was removed and the remaining developer poured into a tray.

Then the canister was refilled with a stop-bath solution that halted any residual development process. A fixative bath followed this and then the negative film was hung on a line to dry. All of this work was done in a darkened environment illuminated only by a battery-powered red-colored "safe-light." In these conditions, Michael soon became expert at developing film.

To make prints, the darkroom operator would simply remove a sheet of photographic paper, lay strips of cut-to-size negatives across it and then sandwich them flat against the paper with a sheet of glass. A bare white light-bulb was allowed to shine through the glass for a few seconds and then the paper was removed.

When developed in an open tray under the safe-light, tiny same-size positive images of the 35mm film soon appeared on the paper. After fixing and proper drying, they could then examine the contact sheets outside in the daylight with the aid of a magnifying lens.

"Look 'ere, there's a bloody wombat!" exclaimed Michael as the three of them sat at the table and studied the photos. There were lots of wallabies, several deer, even a rather large Tasmanian devil, but no pictures of Thylacines.

"Those spotted Fallow deer sure do look good for eating," said Victor with a falsely bored expression. "Maybe I'll snare one and bring it back for fresh meat." The others laughed, thinking Victor was only joking. He wasn't.

A couple of days later, Victor arrived in camp carrying a large bundle. He plopped it down on the table and opened it. Inside, lay the cleaned and butchered remains of a small deer, "a yearling."

"Tonight, we eat good, Kid!" he exclaimed. "Don't worry, Matt, this deer didn't come from any place where any old Thylacine would miss it."

Everyone chuckled at this comment.

While Michael helped Victor prepare the feast, Matthew sat with a cup of tea and watched the two friends joke and banter. Michael's wounds were healing well and he would soon be able to help scout new camera locations when the need became imperative. There was no necessity, though, at least not for several more days. All of the cameras had been visited recently and there was little to do at the moment except to enjoy some leisure time. Perhaps do some reading and a bit of whittling.

"What's that you're carving out of that scrap of wood?" Michael asked Matthew.

"Oh, nothing really, I'm doing it just to occupy my hands."

"Looks a bit like a good luck totem, like something the American Indians used to make... only much smaller," Victor commented as he kneaded some bread dough.

"It's pretty good, though," Michael said, looking at it admiringly. "See here, there's even a little Thylacine carved on top of it."

"Maybe it will bring us some good luck," Matthew laughed, tossing it onto the table.

An hour later, they were treated to grilled venison roasts served with fresh bread and canned vegetables smothered in a kind of cheese sauce.

"Victor, you've completely outdone yourself!" Matthew said in praise. "Say, I've got a bit of Bundaburg rum in my tent that might really go well with this feed."

The big meal and bottle of rum lasted until well past midnight. When the party finally broke up, no one expected to get up early the following morning.

...

During the next several weeks, the weather became increasingly fickle. Sometimes the men would go about their rounds in what almost seemed like

76

tropical warmth. Then, a few days later, they would get out of bed to a light dusting of snow. The unpredictability of Tasmania's weather and the total lack of photographic Thylacine evidence made some days seem exceptionally dreary.

After another darkroom session that had produced nothing more than six wallaby and two deer portraits, the three companions sat in late afternoon "conference" around the big table. Each of them held a mug of coffee and had a hot fresh slice of Victor's camp bread before them.

"I'm going to get fatter than a kangaroo's rear end if I keep eating like this," Michael joked. His arm was healing without infection.

"Me too," Matthew agreed. "Say, I wonder... Perhaps if we <u>fed</u> the Thylacines, we could lure them to the cameras."

"Huh?"

"Well, it's just an idea," he continued. "But some of the old timers used to insist that Thylacines can't be baited into a trap. They said that a Thylacine never eats dead meat or returns to its kill... So what if we use live bait?"

"I mean... Look, wallabies aren't that terribly hard to catch alive and we could rig up some little harnesses to tie them to a tree with. They'd probably be okay for a few days before they needed tending, especially if we left them where there was plenty of feed." Matthew's idea was beginning to take shape.

"We'd also have to reconfigure the camera

setups... move the camera back for a wider view and set the trigger just in front of the wallaby's closest reach. Heck, it just might work."

"It might at that," said Victor after considering the idea for a few moments in silence. "It's certainly worth a try. Nothing else seems to be happening."

"Hey!" Michael interjected suddenly, "I think I hear a chopper." All three men stopped and listened. The "wump, wump, wump" sound of an approaching helicopter could be heard coming across the forest. In a few minutes, the clattering aircraft was hovering above the landing spot that had been selected when the camp was being set up.

"What the hell?" Matthew wondered aloud. "Let's see what's going on."

Standing just outside of the swirl of dust and leaves, they watched the helicopter set down and shut off its engine. When the whirling blades had slowed considerably, the pilot, Sam Strickland, unfastened his seat belt, opened his door and stepped out. Rounding the cockpit, he reached up and opened the passenger door. A slender leg and rounded hip appeared in the doorway as the passenger climbed backwards out of the aircraft.

"Bloody 'ell!" quipped Michael in surprise, "It's a woman."

Full of questions, Matthew stepped forward and greeted his new visitor. "Hello, I'm Matthew Clark. What brings you out this way?"

"Sorry for the surprise. My pilot, Mr. Strickland,

tried to reach you on the radio to let you know that we were coming, but apparently you were out. I'm Patricia Kincaid. I work for the UNESCO World Heritage program and I've got some good news for you, Mr. Clark."

Matthew noted that she spoke with an American accent and seemed to be all business. She was slim, well-dressed and appeared to be in her early thirties. What was she doing here?

"Miss Kincaid, why don't you and Sam come over to camp and have a 'smoko' with us," Matthew suggested hospitably.

"Sorry, I don't smoke," Patricia Kincaid replied tersely.

"I mean... come over and have a 'cupper' and we can talk.

"A cupper?"

"I'm sorry, you've taken me by surprise," Matthew apologized, "That's Australian for, 'Would you care for a cup... a cup of coffee?'"

"Yes, thank you."

With Michael leading the way, the small procession drifted over to the "kitchen" area and the large table. Victor quickly sliced some bread and filled two new mugs with steaming brew. He wore a look of intense amusement on his face.

Sam Strickland seated himself and quietly watched while he idly toyed one of Matthew's wood carvings lying on the table. He too was curious about his new passenger.

"I've come here from New York to review Tasmania's proposed extension to Lake Saint Clair National Park and your department's application for World Heritage Site status," Patricia Kincaid explained in one breath after she had seated herself.

"Miss Kincaid, I don't work for the Parks and Wildlife Service anymore," Matthew responded.

"I know. But I've read your early progress reports and you've done an excellent job. You had the project almost completed before all this 'trouble' began."

"It will take Parks and Wildlife at least another year to finish what you've begun," she continued. "Frankly, there is no one else available with your capability."

"What do you mean by 'no one else'? I'm not available. I'm sure that you probably know by now that I was fired from that project."

"Yes, I realize that. But we need you to help finish the job."

"We?"

"That's why I've come out here; to tell you that I've spoken to the Director's office and they are convinced of your worth. They're asking you to come back."

"Come back?" Matthew shot a concerned glance at Sam. Michael nervously stepped back away from the table and began rolling a cigarette.

"Yes, that is if you will give up this Thylacine business. The Department has assured me that this is all the result of a mistaken sighting that's gotten out of hand."

"And you believed them?!" Matthew asked incredulously.

"Come on, Mr. Clark, everyone knows that these animals are extinct," retorted Patricia Kincaid.

Matthew was beginning to get hot. "I saw one," he said flatly. "What do you say to that?"

"Are you sure?"

"Hell yes, I'm sure!"

"Look, Mr. Clark, there's no need to start swearing. I've got your job back for you."

Both Patricia Kincaid and Matthew were getting red in the face. They stared at each other for a long moment.

"I don't want the bloody job!"

"Are you always so stubborn?"

"G'day, Miss Kincaid. You can make it back to the airport before dark if you leave right now."

"All right, then! Mr. Strickland, shall we go?" asked Patricia Kincaid as she got up and began walking towards the helicopter.

Sam cast a sly smile at Victor and stood up. He was still holding Matthew's wood carving.

"Say, what is this thing?" he asked.

"It's one of Matthew's good luck charms," Victor replied. "He carves them himself."

"Very nicely done..." Sam remarked.

"Take it along with you if you like," Matthew said. "You might need some extra luck with her along."

"Thanks Matthew. Sorry about the

disturbance."

"Don't worry, Sam, it will be all right," Matthew replied, his irritation subsiding. "It's getting dark awfully fast, though. What do you think?"

"I probably could fly back tonight all right, mate, but it might be smarter to wait until morning... 'specially considering who our passenger is and all. Just before we landed, I noticed that there was a big thunderstorm developing in the distance behind us. It might make for some rough flying."

"Well, she is obviously used to getting her own way and certainly won't be happy about staying here," Matthew agreed. "But there's a spare bed in the darkroom tent. You can use that, if you wish. Michael will show you where it is."

"And... I suppose our American guest can stay in my tent. I'll be clearing out for a little 'walk about' tonight. It will only take me a couple of minutes to grab my things and then she can have the place. See ya in the morning, Sam." Matthew was feeling the need for some solitude.

Patricia Kincaid was not pleased when Sam Strickland broke the news to her. After a moment's reflection, though, she nodded her head in compliance to this fate.

"You'll be staying in Matthew's tent tonight, Mam," he added.

"What!?"

"I mean... Matthew has left camp for the night. He said to make yourself comfortable and he'll see us in

82

the morning."

"Okay..." she agreed resignedly.

Matthew left quietly, unobserved by everyone except Michael, and headed for a small rocky plateau not far from camp. Because it jutted abruptly above the trees, he had always thought it might make a nice place to sleep.

Undaunted by the argument, Victor seemed pleased to have guests, especially since one was female. "Care for some supper?" he asked as they gathered once again around the big table.

Michael busied himself by lighting a gas lantern. After a hearty well-cooked meal and a glass of red wine that had been "saved for special occasions," Patricia Kincaid began to feel quite pleasant and talkative. Chatting with Victor, she revealed that she lived alone in a New York City apartment. She had been married once, for several years, but had become a dedicated professional after the divorce. She had not yet had children.

"What's New York like?" asked Michael.

"Well, it's big and very busy. You should go and see it some day. There's nothing quite like the 'Big Apple.'"

The conversation wound on and eventually spotlighted Sam Strickland.

"Yes, I flew for the Royal Australian Air Force in Vietnam," he said.

"See any action?" Victor asked.

"A bit..."

As a chopper pilot, Sam had seen plenty of action and had even been shot down twice behind enemy lines. He had returned home with decorations of military honor. But the public sentiment in Australia, like America's at the time, had been one of rude indifference. It hurt him more than the war did and his return to society had been quite difficult.

These days, Sam projected a personality that seemed both unflappable and exceedingly private. He took good care of himself, though, maintaining his proper weight, appearing to always be ready for action at a moment's notice.

After seeing Patricia Kincaid yawn a couple of times, Victor cordially asked her if he could show her to her quarters. She sleepily agreed.

To the men seated at the big table, watching their female guest's lighted silhouette preparing for sleep a few minutes later, was both a pleasant and exciting experience. Because she hadn't brought any bedclothes, she removed only her jacket and shoes. But when she reached up to extinguish the lantern that illuminated the canvas tent, her firm-breasted shadowy form stopped the men's conversation. For a long moment after the light was out, they continued to stare into the unbroken darkness that contained her tent.

Finally, with a sigh, Victor ended the reverie by saying that it was time for him to turn in. Everyone agreed and soon the big "kitchen" table vanished into the darkness also, as each man found his way to his own bed. However, it was a long time before any of them fell asleep.

When Matthew returned, the morning sun was brightly illuminating the canopy and trunks of the trees surrounding the camp. Around the tents, the ground still lay in retreating shadow. Victor had already served breakfast and everyone was watching two small parrots tug clownishly at opposite ends of a bread-crust. Fascinated by the gemlike quality of their emerald-colored feathers, Patricia Kincaid had failed to notice Matthew's arrival.

"G'day," he announced, trying to be casual.

"Oh, hello," she replied. "Aren't these birds wonderful?"

"They certainly are. I trust you slept well?"

"Yes, thank you."

"Have a spot of coffee, Matt?" Victor asked.

"Thanks, mate."

Matthew sat down and drank the strong brew in silence as Sam gathered Patricia Kincaid's jacket and started for the helicopter. Matthew's wood carving protruded from his hip pocket.

Victor and Michael had just begun to escort the two when she stopped and turned back to Matthew.

"You sure you won't change your mind?" she asked.

"Positive. Have a good life."

Putting her hands on her hips, she gave him a disgusted look and turned towards the waiting men.

"Stubborn!" was the only word he heard her say before she boarded the aircraft.

85

After a few moments, the high-pitched whine of its turbine engine split the serenity of the surrounding wilderness. As the helicopter lifted off, Patricia Kincaid leaned over and peered down at Matthew through the window. With dust and leaves blowing in his face, he silently raised his cup in mock salute.

Chapter Nine

Victor was an expert at snaring animals but he had never tried to capture them alive before. But after several initial failures, his technique began to improve and with Michael's help, they finally devised a padded wire loop that could close around the ankle of a wallaby without injuring it.

Several days earlier, Matthew had radioed for the helicopter, which ferried in new food supplies and two big rolls of poultry netting. They used the wire netting to build a large wallaby cage that had a grassy run for feeding and a walled-off area to allow its inmates some privacy.

Now they were ready to live-catch some wallabies to use as Thylacine bait. Victor and Michael planned to set six snares, while Matthew stayed in camp to finish making some little leather shoulder harnesses that would hold the wallabies to their tethers.

"Good luck to ya, mates!" Matthew called as they left the camp. "You'll need to check those snares first thing in the morning. We have to be as gentle as possible with these animals. They're not as tough as they seem."

He had seen post-capture myopathy before. It had been a serious problem when he was cannon-netting wild kangaroos and wallabies on the mainland for a scientific study paper on their ecology.

Myopathy is a stress-related disease marked by

muscle degeneration and eventual death. Its symptoms usually do not appear until two or three days after the animal had been caught, measured, and released in apparent good health. However, if the animals are handled carefully and immediately upon capture given a large hypodermic dose of Valium, they will usually do quite well.

"You guys have the syringes with you?"

"No worries, mate," Victor laughingly called as he disappeared into the surrounding bush.

When the light of the following morning began to strengthen, it revealed a thickly-furred Bennett's wallaby sitting quietly on its haunches at alert. Its large sensitive ears swiveled this way and that, independently of each other as they sampled the encircling forest for signs of further danger. One of its hind-legs was firmly held in a snare.

With Michael slowly leading the way, the trappers labored up the slope towards the position where the wallaby sat. It had been stopped by the snare over two hours ago on its return from its nightly feeding ground.

At first, it had struggled to near exhaustion; now it sat awaiting its fate. But when the men appeared in the nearby bushes, the animal renewed its escape efforts.

"Hey! We got one here!" Michael cried. "Get out the gunny sack and the 'net.'"

The "net" was little more than three hessian sacks split open and sewed together. Its purpose was to quickly cover the struggling wallaby and subdue it. With a man on each end, it could be pulled over the animal and then pinned to the ground by the weight of one of the men. The other team member would then quickly administer a hypo of Valium through the cloth cover.

After the animal had calmed down and stopped kicking, the burlap cover was then removed and the wallaby grabbed by its tail. Lifting it completely off the ground, it was then gently placed into a hessian sack whose opening was tied off to prevent escape. The animal would soon settle down and allow itself to be carried comfortably over the shoulder of its captor.

The capture team returned to camp just as Matthew was sitting down for lunch. They brought with them two animals in good condition.

"Right-o, mates! Let me try and fit these harnesses on them before they wake up," Matthew cried, ignoring his lunch.

With a little adjusting here and re-sewing there, the harnesses fit perfectly over their small chests. Each had a ring where a restraining line could be tied to it.

"Let's put them in the cage and let 'em recover," Matthew suggested. "Care for a spot of tea?"

Victor heartily agreed; two of these wallabies were rather heavy for one man to carry. Michael's arm was still bandaged.

Over the next three days, two more wallabies were captured and brought into camp. From their seats at the large table, the men could watch them feed on the bundles of grass and leaves that had been put into the cage.

"These Bennett's wallabies seem to take to captivity much easier that most members of the kangaroo family," Matthew observed. "Now, if these animals were Whiptail wallabies, they would have crashed into the fence and killed themselves already."

"Tomorrow, let's move two of the cameras to new locations and put a wallaby into position at each one," he continued. "You guys have any fresh spots picked out?"

"You bet!" replied Victor.

"Good, then today we can go and collect a couple of the cameras from their old locations. With luck, we'll be back before dark."

"If you don't mind, I'll stay behind and do a bit of baking," Michael suggested. His arm was throbbing with pain and he needed rest.

"Good idea, Kid!... see you tonight."

The going was easyYellow Victor and Matthew arrived back in camp just as some sort of Johnny-cake was being removed from the camp oven.

"You guys have perfect timing," Michael humorously observed. The ease of light duty was doing him good.

...

A gentle rain was falling when the three left camp the next morning. Michael carried the harnesses, guy-wires, cameras, hardware, extra clothing, and the lunches in a small backpack, while Victor and Matthew each carried a freshly sacked wallaby.

"They probably don't need the extra Valium, but there's no use in taking a chance on getting them overly excited," Matthew said in preparation to giving each animal another injection.

"Now, now, this won't hurt a bit," Victor gently whispered to a wallaby that had started to struggle in his arms.

"There... nighty, nighty ... that ought to put you into sweet dreamland," Michael cooed in a falsetto voice when the injection was completed.

The first site was six kilometres west of camp towards the Great Pine Tier. Victor had chosen a little wooded grove that seemed to meet Matthew's specifications.

"This is good," he said approvingly after surveying the spot. "Let's set up the camera over there and adjust the zoom lens to wide-angle. The wallaby can be tied to a wire running between those two trees. He'll still be able to move about and feed but he won't be able to get out of camera range."

The camera was secured with screws to a tree trunk and any branches that might obscure its view were removed or bent out of the way. The two flash units were taped into position ten feet on either side of the camera. Two additional units were placed so that they formed the corners of a large imaginary square. When the flashes were triggered, their light would simultaneously radiate towards the center of the square, insuring an even exposure wherever the wallaby happened to be.

This method, known as "X"-flash, is a standard technique for wildlife photography in uncertain lighting conditions. Each flash unit, through electric eye control, is capable of automatically increasing or decreasing the amount of light it projects. By presetting the unit to a particular exposure level rated in F-stops, the amount of light actually flooding the subject will be constant, day or night. The camera lens is then set to the same exposure setting as the flash units.

The infrared trigger was positioned in front of the camera just beyond the furthest reach of the wallaby. The distance between the emitter and the reflector was increased to about six metres, about the same distance as the wallaby's run. Another triggering unit was set up "behind" the wallaby, also just beyond its reach.

When the baited camera trap was nearly complete, the wallaby was removed from its sack and fastened to the wire-run via a short leash clipped to the run and then to the animal's harness. Still groggy from the Valium, the wallaby hopped a few feet, then stopped and began grooming itself.

"Seems right at home," Michael commented.

"Okay, let's test the system," Matthew instructed.

The lens set at wide-angle was focused approx-imately halfway between the two parallel invisible triggering beams. Its increased depth of field would assure that the entire scene would be in focus. Whenever the wallaby advanced toward the camera, it was gently restrained by the leash; when moving toward the trees, it was restrained by stops fastened to the wire of the run.

"Okay, Victor, toss a stick into the forward beam."

Flash, bzzzzt.

Startled, the wallaby flinched slightly and then relaxed.

"Now try the rear beam."

Nothing.

"Hmmmm. Something's wrong. Let's check for loose connections."

"Here's something!" Michael called as he traced the wire from the sending unit to the camera. "Looks like a broken wire."

After the wire was rejoined, the unit worked perfectly.

"Okay... if anything approaches that wallaby from the front or rear, the camera will record it," Matthew said. "Now, let's place a bit of brush around to discourage anything coming in from the side."

By the time they had completed the set, more than half the day was gone. The light rain had slowly diminished into a hazy mist. Although the air was cool and the foliage wet, they found the conditions pleasant for work.

Moving northward towards the "gate," they stopped for lunch when they were about halfway between the two sites.

"Man, am I hungry!" exclaimed Michael. "Let's hope those Tigers - I mean *Thy-la-cines* - are just as hungry. We'll get one for sure."

Matthew smiled at Michael's effort at scientific correctness. Over the past two and a half months, the young man's disposition had changed into an air of contentment. He had mentioned several times that this expedition had "saved" his life.

It was nearly dusk by the time the second camera trap was set up. With Matthew walking in line between them, Victor allowed Michael to guide the party slowly back to camp in darkness.

"We'll have to examine those camera traps first thing in the morning," Matthew said after finishing his supper.

"I'll check the western one; Victor, do you want to inspect the northern one?"

"Sure. I'll even bring a little grass for the wallaby to eat if he's still okay," Victor replied.

"If nothing happens at either of these sites in the next three days, then we should bring the wallabies back here to 'freshen' up in the big cage," Matthew continued. "We can take the other two out as replacements. It would also be a good idea to scout around for a couple of alternate sites."

"We've still got four other cameras to take care of too," Michael commented. "How do you want to handle those for the next few days?"

"If you're up to it, Kid, I'll let you take care of

one or two of them. I don't want you overexerting yourself, though."

"No worries! I'm almost as good as new. Victor took those stitches of his out of my arm several days ago."

"All right then, let's develop whatever exposed film we get as soon as possible."

"Let's hope something happens soon," Victor muttered.

"Getting restless?" asked Matthew.

"Yeah, a bit. We've done a lot of hard work with little result," Victor replied.

...

By the end of a week, the cameras still had recorded nothing more unusual than one of the wallabies breaking free of its harness and escaping. The remaining wallaby was returned to camp and the two "unused" ones were put into place. Victor and Michael were then sent out to trap a couple more wallabies.

Another week went by. Two more wallabies were snared, bringing the total to five. One of the baited cameras was moved to a site just inside the Walls of Jerusalem area along the stream that flowed through the "gate." It took Matthew and Michael nearly all day to complete the setup.

Before returning to camp, Michael led Matthew on a side trip to the base of the cliff where he had been injured to search for some of his belongings that had fallen out of his pack. Unfortunately, very little was recovered.

Since a return trip from base camp was practically an all day hike to this remote camera site, they rotated their duties for the task. Although both of the baited cameras had to be checked every twenty-four hours, the six remaining unbaited camera traps still required only weekly servicing.

For the most part, everyone was kept busy during daylight hours, even if he remained behind in camp. The wallabies had to be fed and watered, batteries need to be charged, film developed, prints made, clothes washed, meals prepared, and equipment serviced or repaired. Evenings usually provided some free-time, though.

Matthew updated his journal and carved wood in his spare time. Victor's gourmet meals, characterized by his knack for improvising, became more imaginative. Michael began playing an old harmonica that his father had given him. Although he was extremely shy about performing in other people's presence, he actually played the instrument quite well. Matthew was wise enough not to say anything about it. After three days, the "old" wallaby was replaced with a "fresh" one at the Walls of Jerusalem site. Victor and Michael serviced the location together that day and took turns carrying the "used" animal back to camp. Michael's injuries had nearly healed.

Tomorrow it would be Matthew's turn to make the long hike up to the "gate" and back. He enjoyed these trips and always found time to explore for twenty or thirty minutes before heading back. He never ceased to marvel at the high walls encircling this land that seemed infinitely dotted with lakes. Each body of water was uniquely colored from a palate that ranged from turquoise to cobalt blue. Though he restrained himself, he often felt like singing when he was here. He did not want to scare the local wildlife.

...

The wallaby was not on his leash when Matthew arrived at the camera site. In fact, the line was broken as if chewed through. About fifteen metres "behind" the rear trigger line, Matthew found the wallaby's remains next to a bush. It had been killed and only partially eaten this morning, probably around daybreak, because the scavenging nocturnal Tasmanian devils had not yet discovered the carcass.

Matthew's heart began to race and his hands trembled slightly as he removed the film cassette from the camera. The frame counter showed that eight exposures had been made. Before leaving the site, he switched off all of the equipment. There was no sense in photographing the brief feeding frenzy that the devils would throw as soon as it became dark, plus it was said that Thylacines never return to their kill.

With the exciting possibility that their quarry had finally been photographed, the return trip back to camp was not much more than a blur of trees and bushes. Michael and Victor were having tea when Matthew arrived.

"Come over and have a bite to eat," Victor called when he saw him. Matthew practically ran to the table.

"Hey guys! I have some film... the wallaby was killed... the rope was broken..." he blurted. Immediately, all food was forgotten.

"Let's develop that film right away," Michael insisted.

All three of them crowded into the darkroom tent as the film was carefully wound onto the plastic reel and placed into the canister. After the various developing, fixing, and rinsing baths were completed, the film was hung up to dry and harden.

"It's going to be a long twenty minutes until that thing is ready for printing," mused Victor.

After the film was dry, the exposed section was snipped away from the unused portion and placed on top of a sheet of photographic paper to make the contact print. The tent became even more cramped because the paper had to be developed and fixed in large flat trays, but no one even considered waiting outside.

An hour and a half after Matthew's return to camp, the prints were ready for viewing.

"Shine that torch right on the images," he instructed. "We'll have to look at them through the magnifying lens."

As Matthew bent over the contact print, carefully examining each frame through the 8x loupe, he saw a progressive series of images showing a familiar striped dog-like animal approach the wallaby from the direction of the camera. As the wallaby attempted to flee, the Thylacine grabbed it in midair and crushed its throat.

The final frame, number eight in the series, showed the animal dragging its prey towards the bush, the tether line stretched tight.

"We have one!" Matthew whooped. "Here, have a look."

Victor took the loupe and examined the images.

"All right!" he exclaimed. "Here, Kid, have a peek at our future fortune!"

"This deserves a drink," Matthew suggested. "I've still got some rum in my tent."

"Hell, let's have a couple of drinks," Victor countered.

"When we're done with that rum of yours, we can try a belt from the bottle of whiskey that I've been savin'." After a pause, he added, "We should start tomorrow's plans."

Chapter Ten

No one slept much that night and all three men were ready to head for the "gate" before daybreak. Each of them carried a backpack filled with equipment and food supplies for several days' stay in the bush. A "replacement" wallaby rode in its gunny sack which was held awkwardly at the carrier's side. Every ten minutes, the sack was passed over for someone else to tote.

It was mid-afternoon by the time they arrived at the camera site. True to their reputation as scavengers, the Tasmanian devils had completely devoured the body of the dead wallaby during the night. Not even a single scrap of broken bone remained.

"I can see why you call them land sharks," Victor said to Michael. "It's a good thing they wait until you're dead before eatin' you."

"They don't <u>always</u> wait," Matthew laughed. "Luckily, you almost never see them in the daytime."

"That's cheering," replied Victor.

The camera setup was moved to a new location about two hundred and fifty metres away. Victor assisted Matthew while Michael, the best tracker in the group, looked for footprints. Before leaving, he mentioned that he might bivouac overnight and meet them at the camera site around 8:30 the next morning.

Victor and Matthew spent the night on the shore of a lake about three and a half kilometres away. When Michael arrived in the morning, he reported that he had not found as much as a single track.

"Well... we can use this place as our field camp," Matthew suggested. "We need to bring in a few more cameras, so why don't we just leave the gear that we're carrying and hike out with empty backpacks? We can break down camera sites numbers two, four, and five... and then grab a couple of wallabies and some more food from base camp. We should be able to get back here around dark or a little later."

Time had suddenly become an important factor to the expedition's success. Each man had his duties to perform and a failure of any part could cause a serious delay in the whole operation. A postponement meant that the Thylacine might leave the vicinity and they would miss it.

Victor disassembled the camera sites and was first to return to the lake camp. About half an hour after dusk, Matthew struggled in with Michael in the lead. Both of them carried full backpacks and a bagged wallaby each. Out of consideration of Michael's injured arm, Matthew carried the heavier load.

By evening of the next day, all of the cameras were fully operational. They were spread throughout a four square kilometre area surrounding the original photo site. Stopping at the lake campsite for lunch, the men began to plan their next move.

"You guys are the best trackers that I know," Matthew told his team. "I suggest that you split up this region between yourselves and go over it with a fine-toothed comb."

102

"Victor," he continued, "why don't you cover the broad area to the north?"

"The 'Kid's' the best tracker," Victor interjected, "I think he would do a better job up there. I'll take the eastern area, it's much smaller."

"That okay with you?" Matthew asked, nodding toward Michael.

"Yep, no worries. I'll swing back around in a couple of days and also have a look at the land between here and the west wall."

"Okay... Then I'll stay and check the wallabies and cameras," Matthew said. "I'll set up a mini film-processing tent here at the lake in my spare time and if I get a chance, I'll go have a look at the land south of here, maybe just outside the 'gate' and beyond."

The men nodded in consent to the plan. They agreed to meet Matthew back at the lake camp on the evening of the third day - sooner, if something were found. Shortly after lunch, both trackers disappeared into the surrounding bush.

For a while, Matthew stood near the lake, watching the swirl of some unseen creature swimming beneath the water's surface.

Most likely it's a platypus, he thought. These improbable animals were actually quite common in Tasmania, ranging from high altitude lakes down to the lowland rivers. Then, for a half-second, a rubbery bill and furry head broke the water's surface. It was indeed a platypus.

Sucking in his breath, he began the task of

sorting out the equipment. First, he set up a "kitchen" area where he could cook meals away from the breezes. There would be no campfire here, just a small petrol stove that produced no smoke and left no trace. Everyone in the expedition carried one now.

After heating some water for tea, Matthew extracted the mini-darkroom tent from its storage bag and pondered its assembly. After erecting its collapsible metal frame, he then attached to it a small, cramped, black-colored cloth room measuring about a metre and a half square and a metre and a half high.

When at last it finally seemed to stand properly, Matthew climbed into the cubicle and zipped himself in. The door had a double closure to insure that all light from outside was excluded. A torch-light fitted with a red filter, however, allowed him to see.

Fortunately, he was not claustrophobic because there was absolutely no room to spare inside - just enough to squat over his chemicals - but it would do the job. Baffled vents along the bottom and in the ceiling allowed him enough fresh air to keep breathing.

Matthew checked both wallaby sites the next morning after sunrise. Neither camera had exposed any film and the wallabies were grazing peacefully when he arrived. This was a disappointment. It indicated that the Thylacine may have already moved out of the area.

Deciding to leave the unbaited cameras alone until tomorrow, he walked slowly southward in a wide zigzag pattern with his attention focused on the ground. In one location where two animal trails crossed, he found an interesting footprint. However, after several minutes of careful scrutiny, he finally decided that it was only the half-formed spoor of a Tasmanian devil.

Later in the afternoon, along a muddy portion of trail about one-hundred and fifty feet inside the "gate," Matthew found another set of footprints. These were clearly different from anything he had seen before. Although they resembled a dog's prints, they were more elongated and had smaller pads.

Tucked in his notebook, he had a drawing of a Thylacine footprint that he had photocopied from a museum paper. Victor and Michael also carried copies of the print. Matthew took out the paper and compared it to the footprint on the ground. They matched perfectly.

Dropping to the ground on his hands and knees, he intently studied the footprint. Judging from its present condition of weather-decay, it had probably been made two nights ago. Remaining on all fours, Matthew crawled beside the trail until he came to another print and then another.

Excitement began to well up in him until beads of sweat formed on his brow. The Thylacine footprints led him down to the "gate" and then through it. Then, about thirty metres south of the gap, they abruptly disappeared.

After a careful study of the area, Matthew was unable to determine where or in which direction the animal had gone. He continued to search, though, until gathering dusk forced him to give up.

Back in camp, Matthew ate a quick meal and then crawled into his swag. Sleep seemed evasive. His mind reeled with questions and possibilities.

Where had the Thylacine gone? Would it come back? Where was its den? Did it even use a den? Did it have a mate? What had Victor or Michael found during their searches?

Victor and Michael weren't due back until the end of the next day. Until then, Matthew had to continue searching for tracks alone... unless the animal killed one of his wallabies that evening.

Matthew woke abruptly at dawn. He had fallen asleep sometime in the middle of the night when his train of thought finally petered out. He wanted to go check the cameras immediately but knew that he needed to wait until mid-morning when it was certain that the nocturnal wildlife "shift" in activity had ended. From this period on, until just before sunset, most night-active animals were asleep and there was little chance that he would surprise a Thylacine out hunting. Reluctantly, he cooked himself a leisurely breakfast and prepared for an active day.

Again, the wallabies were untouched. Matthew supplied them with food and water and then moved on to check the unbaited camera traps. The film had advanced in both of them.

Replacing the film with fresh cassettes, he hurried back to camp to develop them. The darkroom cubicle seemed even more cramped than before and the film processing appeared to take almost forever. When it was finally done, the photographs were disappointing... just a deer and three wild wallabies.

"Damn!"

Hurrying back through the gate, Matthew quickly located the spot where he had quit tracking the night before. Finding nothing more, he began to range outward from that point in ever-widening concentric circles. By late afternoon, he still had not found any new prints.

Frustrated, he headed back to camp and his rendezvous with Victor and Michael. They were waiting when he arrived.

"Hello! How 'ja do?" Matthew called in greeting.

"Neither one of us found anything," Victor replied. "We might as well be chasing a ghost."

"I found some tracks, but I lost them," Matthew said.

"Where?!" both trackers asked in unison.

"Down south, by the 'gate.' Listen, Michael, I'll take you over there first thing in the morning. Victor can join you later, after he's tended to the wallaby camera sites."

"While you blokes look for footprints, I'll go down to base camp, pick up some more grub, and carry a couple of live traps up here," Matthew continued. "I think it's time that we started setting them up. Who knows? We just might get lucky."

The next day, Matthew left Michael at the "gate" and began the hike back to base camp. Almost immediately, Michael found several more Thylacine footprints and began following them... but they ended again after only a few metres. Squatting on his haunches, Michael carefully studied the ground around him. He found little to indicate the direction the animal had taken, except that the tracks were headed southwest when they disappeared.

This then became the general bearing that Michael would range in as he studied each broken twig and crushed leaf on the ground's surface. If a clue existed as to where this elusive animal had gone, he would most likely find it.

Base camp had been undisturbed by visitors since the team had been away. Matthew quickly filled his backpack with foodstuff and then lashed two fold-down live traps over the top of the pack. The load was rather unwieldy due to the large size of the traps, but fortunately it was not heavy. After having a bite to eat, he began the long hike back up to the "gate."

It was extremely slow going in places where the brush was thick because branches tended to get caught in the mesh of the traps. Every few moments Matthew was forced to stop and extricate himself. At this pace, he knew that he would not make it back to the camp by the lake before dark.

In the late afternoon, about ten kilometres before the "gate," he removed the cumbersome pack and took a breather by a shallow stream that crossed the faint trail he was following. Sitting on an exposed tree root that twisted crazily across the ground, he wiped his forehead on his sleeve and followed the watercourse with his eyes up to the narrow gully from which it flowed. He was thinking about making camp for the night when, about twenty metres away, he noticed a clear rivulet flowing down a rock face and into the stream.

"Aha, must be a spring!... I could use a good cold drink," he told himself. The water gushed from a fissure in the rock and tumbled through a series of small mossy pools before joining the larger current. Placing his hands on either side of one of the larger pools, he bent down to the water's surface and sucked the cool liquid through his lips. It tasted extremely good and was very refreshing.

Chapter Eleven

As Matthew raised his head from the pool, his eyes met the quiet gaze of another being staring at him from within a nearby bush. At first, the eyes did not seem to be connected to a face, then Matthew noticed the creature's narrow muzzle and short pointed ears. There was a kind of odd serenity about the animal that impressed the man. He had seen this face before... he was looking at a Thylacine.

Before Matthew could take another breath, the orbs vanished, the opening in the bush suddenly closing like a shutter. Springing to his feet, Matthew tried to cut off the animal's escape. It was too late; all he got was a brief glimpse of a stiff tail vanishing around a bend in the gully.

Forgetting his backpack and equipment, he began tracking the fleeing animal as best he could. The stream flowed through moss and rock substrates, but occasionally he would find a stray footprint in muddy patches as he followed it upward. Eventually, it led him to a small soggy plain covered with spiky Button- grass interspersed with huge ferns.

This was an area of whose existence Matthew had not been aware. After examining the map that he carried folded in his pocket, he reckoned that he must be somewhere due east of the "gate." It was dusk by the time he returned to his backpack so he decided to bivouac right there.

Daylight seemed a very long time in coming and Matthew was already on his feet before the first hint of dawn. He had plenty of breakfast food with him but was forced to eat it cold. He had left both his tent and the little gas-fired camp stove back at the lake and did not dare to light a cooking fire. The smell of smoke might drive his quarry even further away.

When it was light enough to travel, he made his way back to the stream and began setting up the traps, one up on either side of the creek. Each was placed in such a way as to force any medium-sized animal following the stream to go into it. Both ends of the trap were open, creating the illusion that the creature could easily pass through. Those ends, however, instantly closed once an animal was inside.

After camouflaging the traps and blocking any alternate routes around them with leafy branches, Matthew shouldered his pack and carefully retraced his steps back up to the ferny plain. Unfortunately, he discovered nothing new on the way.

Near the middle of the expanse was a small moss-covered knoll that offered a view of the surroundings from its top. Matthew climbed it to have a look around. To the north, the land was much more broken by rock outcrops and he knew that it would eventually terminate into the sheer southeast cliff that enclosed the Walls of Jerusalem area. In the direction of the "gate," the forest seemed to become much wetter and more dense. To the northeast, a small creek flowing into the sodden plain quickly vanished among the ferns and Button-grass. Not knowing which way to go, Matthew decided to follow the stream, perhaps to see its source.

The headwaters were formed by a series of small springs issuing from the base of a rocky ridge. In the protected cirque formed by the ridge, he noticed several kinds of plants that he had never seen before. One, a monstrous fern, had fronds more than eight metres long. Another was a climbing vine that bore large sky blue pea-like blossoms with black centers. Fascinated by this find, he stopped to collect specimens and to make some notes and drawings.

Perhaps, he thought, *I have discovered a lost refuge for these unusual species.*

His search of the immediate vicinity suggested that he could be right. These plants seemed to only grow within the protection of this rocky cirque. Forgetting about the Thylacine temporarily, Matthew decided to explore the nooks and crannies of every gully and rock outcrop he came to. Eventually, his search led him to the head of the cirque.

Wondering what lay beyond the ridge, he decided to scale it. The way up was steep and slippery with broken cobble, but after a couple of hours of scrabble-climbing, he finally stood on the knifelike summit of the ridge. Looking down, Matthew could see that the back side of the slope, also covered in broken rock, terminated in a boulder and tree-lined gully far below.

After carefully descending the steep rock face of

113

the ridge crest, he took three steps on the cobble scree and lost his balance. He slid at least twenty or thirty metres before he was able to stop himself.

"Rats! I'm not going to be able to go back up that way. Well, at least I'm not hurt."

Matthew slowly picked his way downward through the scree, slipping and sliding every few steps. Sometimes he would skid several metres before managing to get stopped again.

Just before reaching the gully, however, he slid out of control and crashed into a large boulder. His right ankle was badly bruised and his leg received a nasty gash. When he finally reached stable ground again, he stopped to bandage his wound and try to compose himself.

"Damn the luck!" he hissed. "At least there's no broken bones or severed arteries... that much is good."

A thin trickle of water threaded its way through the boulder-strewn gully.

This probably leads back to the other creek, he reasoned, partly in blind hope. *In any case, I'll follow it down until I clear the ridge. Then I can swing back to the base of the cirque and get the heck out of here.*

Matthew knew that he had better start moving soon before his leg stiffened up from the injury. As long as he kept on walking, it would stay reasonably limber.

The rock-filled gully offered no path to walk along, so progress was painfully slow. Fortunately, the worst of it ended when the gully widened out into moist lowland covered with more Button-grass. The tiny stream Matthew had been following was now much larger, its strength apparently increased by hidden springs.

...

He saw the footprint just as he was crossing over from one bank to the other. Perfectly imbedded in an exposed mud bar in the middle of the rivulet was a fresh Thylacine print. He dared not move his feet for fear of stepping on another one and obliterating it. So, poised in mid-stride, Matthew stood stock-still and looked carefully around for more tracks. To his left he saw another, and then another and still another.

Following the tracks downstream, he finally came to a place that was fairly riddled with tracks all around. A narrow, but well-defined trail led away from the creek and towards a rocky incline. Matthew followed it uphill. When he reached the base of the slope, his heart skipped a beat and then began to race. In the fault zone where two huge slabs of rock had slipped past each other during a brief moment of geological activity thousands of years ago, a small triangular-shaped cave had been created. The ground around its entrance had been worn smooth by passing feet.

Although it was too small for him to enter, Matthew knew that he had discovered the Thylacine's den. Unable to squat because of his leg injury, he stared into the entrance on his hands and knees. Small whimpering sounds issued from the hole.

"What the...?"

Carefully, he stuck his head into the hole and listened. At first he heard a scuffling noise and then a series of little whines.

My god! It sounds like there's pups in there. I think I've found a den with baby Thylacines in it!

He continued to listen for another ten minutes. There were definitely pups somewhere inside.

Where are the parents? I mustn't scare them away.

Realizing that he might be putting the pups at risk of abandonment, Matthew quickly withdrew his head and turned to leave. The increased adrenaline flow caused by his excitement seemed to strengthen him. Now, at least, he didn't notice the pain when he quickened his stride. He felt that he needed to hurry and tell the others what he had found.

Within another five kilometres, the creek joined the stream that he had been following earlier that morning. Upstream, about a half a mile away to his left, rose the cirque with the unusual plants growing at its base. His guess about the direction of the rivulet's flow had been right.

Two discoveries - the Thylacines and the plants of the cirque - in one day. It was amazing. A field biologist's dream come true.

"I've got to get back as soon as possible and tell the guys!" he thought out loud as he began following the watercourse back down to the soggy plain.

By the time he had crossed the muddy expanse, it was nearly dark. Matthew halted for the night on the edge of the sodden prairie, along the stream that led to where he had set the traps.

His leg was stiff and swollen when he woke the next morning. It took several minutes of limping before he could even stand properly. After changing the dressing on his leg and snacking on a spare "energy bar" that he discovered in his pack, Matthew retraced his route back to the traps. They were untouched.

I guess I can just leave these here until I get back with Victor and Michael, he thought.

Matthew continued on for a few steps, but then a sudden thought checked him.

This may be the only chance that anyone in the world will ever get to study these animals in the wild... and there are pups in there. That means I have located a family of them.

An unexpected wave of anxiety washed over Matthew, rendering him unable to move forward.

If I go back and tell them about this, my guys will tear that hill apart to capture those animals. Any opportunity for research will be lost forever. I seriously doubt if they would allow me even two days of study before we catch them. It's been hard enough just to find a footprint of one.

His head pounding from the pain of his dilemma, Matthew dropped his pack to the ground, sat down beside it and put his face into his hands. Several minutes passed before he raised his head again. He knew what he had to do. He could not tell the men what he had found, at least not for a while. This would buy him some time, even if it were just a day or two in which to study the animals.

117

"I'll come back and put up the small tent and use it for an observation blind," Matthew told himself. "Then maybe I can learn something about how they live." He felt strongly that it was the right thing to do.

After folding up the traps and lashing them to his pack again, he gathered up the small branches that he had cut for camouflage and shoved them under a large bush. Because he knew that for the next week or two, Victor and Michael would easily be able to "read" what had happened here, he tried not to leave anything that would draw their attention to this spot.

It was late afternoon by the time Matthew reached the "gate" and nearly dark when he arrived at the camp by the lake. Because of his injured leg and the awkward load, it had been very slow going.

"Hello!" Michael greeted Matthew upon his arrival. "Let me help get that pack off of you. We thought something had happened..."

It was then that he noticed Matthew's limp and bloodstained trousers.

"Let me have at look at that, Matt," said Victor. "Kid, would you mind bringing the light over here?"

"Well, it's not as bad as it looks," Matthew replied.

"That cut's a bit deep but it's been bandaged and kept clean. Your ankle looks a bit rough, though," Victor commented. "How'd you do it?"

"Lost my footing on a slick spot and smashed into a boulder."

"Yeh. That's easy to do out here," Victor said.

"It's a wonder that it doesn't happen more often. You hungry?"

Matthew nodded that he was and tried to rise to his feet.

"Hey, don't bother getting up. We'll bring the food over to you. You need some rest."

As he ate, Matthew asked the men what they had seen since he had been away.

"I've gone all over that area by the "gate" and haven't found much more than what you did the other day," replied Michael.

"Not much results from the camera stations either," Victor added. "...and I think we should probably catch a couple of new wallabies for bait. The two that we're using haven't been getting much to eat lately and we ought to replace them."

"Yes, you are right," Matthew agreed. "But let's talk about what we should do in the morning after I've had a bit of sleep. Okay?"

"Sorry... you do look like you need some rest, Matt."

Matthew uttered an audible sigh as he crawled into his sleeping bag. He was damned tired and he needed some time to think about how he was going to keep his men busy without revealing his find.

For several moments, Matthew pondered whether or not any results gained from studying the Thylacines would be worth the effort of such deception. "It would only be for a few days..." he told himself as he fell asleep.

Chapter Twelve

Morning came all too soon. Luckily, Victor had a cup of strong coffee ready for Matthew as soon as he had stumbled to his feet. His leg throbbed with pain.

"Well, how do you think we ought to proceed?" Matthew asked after swallowing a few gulps of the steaming brew. He had been unable to form a plan.

Victor spoke first, "Let's get those traps you brought with you into service as soon as possible. I think we're getting close to our quarry now."

"We can move a few of the cameras around to new sites too," added Michael.

"Well, you blokes sound pretty positive," Matthew said. "So let's see how we'll split the work."

"How's yer leg this mornin'?" asked Michael.

"Better, but I should probably take it easy for another day," Matthew replied. "But I can help you with the cameras." It was exactly the opposite of what he really wanted to do, but he needed time... time to heal, and to think.

"You sure you can hike?" Victor asked.

"They'll be no worries as soon as I get limbered up. I'll carry just the lunch, you can carry the rest," Matthew added while winking at Michael. "Victor, why don't you snare us some fresh wallabies and set up those traps? As soon as I'm feeling better, I'll make a slow and easy hike back to base camp and bring up the other two traps." Matthew felt that there was more than enough work to keep these guys occupied for the next week.

"Sounds good, Matt!" Victor agreed. "I have a feeling that it won't be much longer until we have this 'cat' in the bag."

After breakfast, Victor disappeared with the two traps and some snares. Michael insisted that Matthew stay in camp and rest his leg while he inspected the first three cameras. When he protested, Michael told him teasingly that these were his "orders." Secretly, Matthew relished this unexpected time alone; he could think things through and prepare his gear for the return trip to base camp with a "side trip" to the den site.

Close to midday, Michael breathlessly returned, brandishing two rolls of film. "One of the wallabies got trashed last night!" he exclaimed. "Let's get this film developed and see what happened."

Instead of being elated by this news, Matthew felt uneasy. Actually, he wanted to capture a Thylacine but was worried that they would be caught before he had a chance to study them.

"A few days observation could double the world's knowledge about these elusive animals," Matthew told himself.

An hour and a half later, they climbed out of the portable darkroom with two contact prints in hand. One depicted the usual passing deer and a wallaby, the other was a scene of predation. In only four frames, a Thylacine rushed in from behind the camera, caught the poor tethered wallaby by the throat, and dragged it out

122

of camera range.

"Let's look for prints, Michael, while they're still fresh."

"I have, but this animal is smart and keeps to the rocks. I lost him less than a hundred feet from the camera site, both coming and going."

"Well then, check the rest of the cameras today and tomorrow you and Victor can move this camera to another site and get it ready for a new wallaby."

"Yes-sir!"

...

One other camera had recorded some movement and Matthew planned to develop the film immediately.

"Why don't you sit for a spell, and let me 'soup' it?" Michael suggested.

"Well, okay... I'll make some tea. Care for a cup?"

It was after dark when Michael emerged from the tiny darkroom. The contact printed showed only a single deer as it grazed slowly across the camera's field of view. It seemed to have ignored the flashes and whir of the camera's motor because it did not even raise its head once during the photo session.

"Bugger all!" Michael exclaimed. "This deer's a camera hog. If he keeps this up, we'll have 'im for tea, too."

Victor arrived late and listened to the news.

"Okay, I'll help you get that new camera site set

up and we'll trap some fresh wallabies as soon as possible," he said. "See, Matt, I told you things would start happenin'."

"Okay guys, I'm turning in," Matthew said. "My leg feels better and we need to get an early start tomorrow."

Victor was right, things were beginning to happen. There seemed to be an excited "buzz" in the air. After nearly four months of hard work, the camp was filled with a feeling that success was just around the corner.

Two days later, Matthew left the lake camp at first light. Ostensibly, he was headed back to base camp again to pick up the remaining two live traps. By four o'clock in the afternoon, however, he was following the little creek that crossed the trail up to the fern plain. It was practically dark by the time he reached the Thylacine's gully. This time he had brought all the camping gear that he needed, including the nylon dome-shaped tent that he normally used when away from base camp.

After erecting the pop-up tent some one hundred metres away from the animal den site, Matthew quickly retreated back down the gully and climbed a huge shoulder of rock. He planned to spend the night here while the Thylacines investigated his empty tent. With luck, by morning they would have accepted it as a harmless part of the environment.

There were tracks all around the tent when Matthew examined it the next morning. He had impatiently waited until after ten o'clock and the sun was high when he felt sure that the Thylacines would not be active.

To finish preparing his hide, he first lifted the whole tent off the ground and carried it intact to a point only fifty metres or so from the den site. From here, he could get a good view of the entrance. Then, after filling his water bottles in the little creek, he unzipped the tent and slipped his equipment and himself inside. Arranging his things to make himself as comfortable as possible, Matthew could peer through a small screened window at the den. There was still no sign of activity.

After watching the den for about ten minutes, Matthew slumped to the tent's floor and let the heat of the midmorning sun put him to sleep. As long as he remained here, he knew that he would have to get his sleep during the day and be awake all night like the nocturnal Thylacines.

It was early evening during the hour of golden light when something caused Matthew to sit up and become alert. Perhaps it was a noise or some sort of sixth sense, he didn't know... but as he gazed out of the little window, he saw an adult Thylacine walk slowly, very hesitatingly up the path towards the den. When it reached the lair, it stopped and looked directly at the tent. Matthew instinctively "froze" and even stopped breathing for a moment.

Satisfied that the new object in his neighborhood was not an immediate threat, the Thylacine turned its head and disappeared into the den.

125

A chorus of squeaky sounds issued from its unseen depths. Matthew's handwritten notes frantically recorded the event.

It became too dark to see after nightfall; the moon was not due to rise until long after midnight. Although Matthew attempted to stay awake all night, he could not manage the task. He dozed for long stretches of time, sitting in his observer's position... fits of wakefulness, then sleep returning... dawn approaching.

Again he woke with a jolt, as if on cue. Another Thylacine, this one slightly larger, was carrying the leg of a wallaby in its jaws. Upon hearing the slight sound of Matthew shifting his weight in order to get a better view, it also stopped and listened carefully. Then it approached the den, dropped the meat at its "doorstep" and yawned widely.

A smaller animal, presumably the female, appeared at the entrance. Two roly-poly pups immediately followed her. As soon as the pups saw the wallaby leg, they bit into it and excitedly tugged each other back and forth while venting high-pitched squeals.

After the two adults sniffed each other's muzzle in greeting, the larger animal lay down beside the pups in a posture of comfortable relaxation. Approaching the severed wallaby leg, the female Thylacine placed her left forepaw on top of it, bent down and started chewing off small chunks of meat with her carnassial teeth. The pups eagerly grabbed and swallowed every small piece that was dropped for them. When the pups' enthusiasm for food finally waned, the female then ate her fill and flopped down beside her mate.

"During the (apparent) weaning process, the parents feed the pups by biting off small pieces of meat..." Matthew hastily wrote in his notes. He was deliriously happy. It was very possible that no human before him had ever seen what he had witnessed this morning.

For a long while, the pups rolled and chased each other in the short grass while the parents rested. Just as he was beginning to wonder whether or not the pups were completely weaned, they both approached their mother and began to nurse.

I guess that answers that! he noted.

As the morning progressed, the Thylacine family continued to loaf in front of their den. Growing thirsty, Matthew shifted his position in order to reach the water bottle. The sounds of his rustling brought immediate attention from the adult Thylacines. However, neither one of them bothered to get up. After a few moments, they diverted their attention to the pups, who were playing a few yards away. It was an idyllic scene.

Suddenly, one of the adults let out a cough-like bark and leapt to its feet. In a flash, both pups scuttled into the den, their parents quickly following them. For an instant, Matthew thought that he had unconsciously done something to scare them. A second later, though, a large shadowy form flashed through the air and headed towards the den. It was a Wedge-tailed eagle.

127

Banking upward at the bottom of its dive, the huge bird swerved to narrowly miss a small tree and soared out of the scene. Apparently, it had just made a try for one of the Thylacine pups.

Matthew waited for over an hour for the Thylacines to reappear. Tiring of this, he finished his breakfast, drank a swig of water and lay down for a nap. It was mid-afternoon before he woke. Opening a bag of biscuits and a cold can of pork and beans, he silently ate his meal. Soon it would be time for the adult Thylacines to go hunting.

For two days and nights, Matthew stayed in the tent watching the activities of the Thylacine family. By now, he was able to recognize each individual and to get a sense of its personality. The big male was very tolerant and allowed the youngsters to playfully pull his tail and nip his ears.

The female, on the other hand, would not let the pups pester her. They were allowed to approach her closely only when nursing and then just for short periods of time. Clearly, it seemed, she was in the process of weaning them.

For the most part, life in the tent was a tedious rhythm. This was offset only by the brief times Matthew was able to see the Thylacines. Each day at midmorning, he would sneak out to relieve himself at a "toilet" spot a few hundred metres away. His "deposits" were always carefully covered with soil before he returned to the tent. On the way back, he washed his unshaven face in the creek and refilled his water bottles.

At night, he used an empty bottle to store his urine.

By the third day, Matthew's notebook was literally filled with remarks and most of his scanty food supplies were gone. It was time to continue on to base camp and pick up more supplies and the remaining two traps. Before leaving, however, he erected a teepee of branches around the tent, screening it from the Thylacine den. Then he rolled up the tent and secured it to his backpack. The woodsy curtain would make the tent's absence and reappearance less obvious to the animals. He would need that tent at the lake camp and planned to bring it back with him when he returned to continue his study.

After being unoccupied for several weeks, base camp was showing signs of deterioration. Fallen leaves covered the big table, a box of stores had been torn open by some small animal looking for food and a broken tree branch had ripped through the roof of his tent. It took Matthew most of the day to repair the damage and tidy the place up.

He arrived back at the lake camp with the two live traps and his pack bulging with food just after dark the following day. His leg had healed well during his stay at the den site and he had made good time on his return trip.

"Hey-ho, mates!" Matthew called to Victor and Michael. "How's it been going?"

Michael rushed over to help Matthew remove his pack.

"We've caught five wallabies and not much

else," Victor replied. "It won't be long, though... I just feel it."

"You were out a bit longer than we expected... did you meet some trouble on the trail again?" asked Michael.

"Not a bit... I just took it slow and easy on the way down. Base camp was in a bit of a mess when I arrived, though, and I had to repair a big hole in my tent."

"What happened, Matt?" Victor asked.

"Nothin' much, just a big ol' Snow gum branch broke off and fell through it."

"Is everything else okay?"

"Yeah, no worries, I tidied the place up before I left. Brought lots of grub with me... help me get these traps out of the way, Michael, and I'll unpack it."

There were the usual canned goods, some flour for making pan bread, a bit of sugar and coffee, and a small bottle of Bundaburg rum.

"Feel like warming up your bones a bit?" Matthew asked as he opened the bottle and offered it to Michael.

"Sure!"

The bottle was passed around until it was empty. When the talk began to fade, Matthew erected his dome-tent, tossed in a sleeping bag and crawled inside. He was asleep in less than a minute.

Victor did not know why, but he had a vague feeling that Matthew was not telling him everything. He didn't know what it was, but he was sure that something wasn't quite right. Long ago he had learned to follow his instincts and not to question any doubts that crept into his mind. All he could do at the moment, though, was to wait and see what revealed itself.

Chapter Thirteen

Two of the five wallabies that Victor had caught were tethered at camera sites; the rest had been released. In the morning, after the new traps were assembled, Michael and Matthew took one out to be set. Victor took the other trap.

Because Matthew already knew where the Thylacines were, it was difficult to go through the motions of pursuit. At that moment, he desperately wanted to be back at the den studying them, not running around setting traps. On the other hand, he needed to be cautious about leaving the Walls of Jerusalem area too soon. It may raise some hard-to-answer questions and he did not want to have to lie to the men. So, for the next few days, he would carefully keep his notebook out of sight and wait for an excuse.

"We're still not gettin' results," Matthew announced on the morning of the fourth day. "We're going to lose the animals if they move out of this area."
"Animals? Do you reckon there's more than one?" asked Michael.

"It's quite possible, unless the tracks we saw earlier were made by a lone wanderer."

"Victor, I think it's time we got a little more aggressive," Matthew said. "I want you to do another three day circle around this area and look for fresh tracks."

"Michael, I would like you to continue checking

the live traps and camera setups. I'll do some tracking
myself, outside the gate on my way back to base camp."

"Why are you going there?" asked Victor.

"There's a trammel net there and it might come
in handy should we actually catch or corner one of
these critters. Also, I can bring in another load of
foodstuffs."

"Well, Michael's an excellent hiker, maybe he
should..." Victor began.

"I'd rather do it myself," Matthew interrupted.
"We'll need Michael's tracking talents if a Thylacine
comes a' calling on one of our wallabies in the night."

"Yeah, I guess you're right..." Victor agreed after
a moment's hesitation.

By the time Matthew crawled out of his sleeping
bag the next morning, Victor had already gone.
Michael, leaning on a moss-covered rock, was drinking
a cup of coffee and watching the wind ripple the lake.
He was waiting for the midmorning lull in wildlife
activity before going out to check the cameras.

"G'day, Michael," Matthew greeted him. "Got
any more of that coffee?"

"Yes-sir! Comin' right up."

"It's just a matter of time before we're rich, don't
you reckon?" Michael asked.

"Let's not start counting our money just yet,
Kid."

"Yeh, I know... but it's just that I have this
feeling that we're gonna win."

Shouldering his pack, Matthew wished Michael

good luck and headed south towards the "gate." After passing through it, he turned onto the game trail that they used to cross the first range of hills. This route helped him to avoid a large area of nearly impenetrable scrub.

After walking over fallen logs and balancing on slippery rocks for about three hours, Matthew stopped for a break and looked around for a place to sit. As he approached an inviting rock, a deadly Tiger snake more than five feet long and as thick as his wrist, rose its head as if to strike if he came any nearer. Matthew abruptly halted, then backed off.

Ooops!

Giving the snake a respectfully wide berth, he resumed his trek. During the mating season, these dangerous animals become boldly territorial and there was little chance of surviving a bite without medical help.

Upon reaching the little stream that led up to the ferny plain, Matthew stopped for another breather. For some reason, at that moment he suddenly developed the strongest feeling that someone, or something, was following him.

"I'll continue on down the main trail for another half an hour until I find a lookout. If there's anybody following me, I ought to be able to see or hear 'em," he told himself.

He found a good observation spot on a brushy rock outcrop that overshadowed the path. From his vantage point, he could see a good section of the track as it threaded along a gully. After an unprofitable hour's wait, however, Matthew decided that the feeling of being pursued must have been just his imagination.

He was feeling a bit guilty about misleading his men and was having second thoughts about what was the right thing to do. He knew, though, that he must learn as much as he could about these wonderful animals... before it was too late.

Returning to the trail, Matthew followed it back to the small stream. As he turned and began to trace it upward to the fern plain, again he had the feeling that someone was following him. This time, the sensation was more certain.

Leaving the creek behind him, Matthew bushwhacked his way cross-country along a compass bearing for three kilometres, then turned ninety degrees and continued the course for another kilometre. The feeling did not go away.

He changed his direction again, this time back towards the creek. A half kilometre from where the stream flowed out of the fern plain, he finally halted under a huge tree with fort-like buttressed roots. He was beginning to feel safe again. It was also growing late and he needed to eat. Like most of his meals on the trail lately, he ate this one cold, washed down with a drink of water.

Using the tent as a ground cloth, Matthew then unrolled his sleeping bag between two of the massive roots and crawled in. For a while, he listened to the evening sounds, trying in vain to discern anything

136

unusual. At last he fell into a fitful sleep. Unbeknownst
to him, Victor also was hunkering down for the night
not more than two hundred metres away. He had
followed Matthew out of mixture of curiosity and
suspicion.

...

Morning arrived cold and rainy. Matthew spent
little time breaking camp and was soon slogging his way
across the small plain. Around noon, the rain slackened
into fine mist. By the time he arrived at the den site, the
sky was beginning to show patches of deep afternoon
blue. After filling his water bottles in the creek, he
quickly set up the tent and moved in. Matthew
fervently hoped that his return would not disturb the
Thylacines. Just before sunset, he learned that it hadn't.

The entire family appeared at the entrance of
the den. After a few moments of unsuccessful nuzzling
for milk, a light nip from the female sent both
youngsters retreating back inside. Then, with the male
in the lead, both adult animals left together in the same
direction.

Matthew remembered having read stories
related by old-timers that Thylacine pairs would often
hunt together, just like wolves. Apparently they were
right. There was no further activity at the den until
morning.

While he watched and waited, Matthew felt a
strong twinge of sadness. He knew that he had a
contractual obligation to trap them, but in his heart he

fervently wished for these animals' continued freedom. They deserved at least that much from the world.

...

Dawn's blue light had already been sublimated by the orange glow of daybreak when both parents arrived together. This time, the female was in the lead. Behind her, the male wearily carried a small wallaby in his mouth. The female went directly into the den, while the male dropped his load and waited outside.

In a few moments, the two pups tumbled out of the entrance and seized the wallaby. Then both parents laid down and watched the pups attempt to chew off pieces of meat. After a while, the female stood up and began tearing bits of flesh from the wallaby carcass.

Suddenly, when both pups and the parents dashed into the den, Matthew knew that something had frightened them. Instead of another eagle attack which he had expected, he was extremely surprised to see Victor, angry and ready for a fight.

As soon as Matthew came to, beaten and bruised, he groggily crawled into his ransacked tent. Here he discovered that his precious field notes were missing. Even though he could hardly sit up, he knew that he must do something. Victor was a loose cannon. Who knows what other damage he might do? At first light, Matthew would go to base camp and use the radio to call for help.

PART TWO

Chapter Fourteen

Except for a water bottle and a few granola bars
tossed into his day pack, Matthew abandoned the rest of
his camping equipment. He was still rather wobbly and
carrying even this small weight bothered him. After an
hour of limping down the trail, he began to limber up a
little but his left eye remained swollen shut.

As he neared the base camp that evening, he
crept towards its perimeter as stealthily as he could, just
in case Victor was there. The camp was empty... no
one had heard him stumble and break a branch with a
loud "snap."

However, someone had been in camp earlier
that afternoon. The cooking fire was still smoldering
and the place looked like a cyclone had recently swept
through it. Almost all of the boxes of stored supplies
had been ransacked. Flour and tin cans were scattered
everywhere. More importantly, the trammel net was
missing.

Matthew hastily went to his tent. Its interior
was also in shambles. The big two-way radio was
smashed and his packet of business papers detailing the
agreement with Yeoh Chin Choo was gone.
A hypodermic kit containing knockout serum was also
missing. He now knew exactly what Victor was

planning to do.

Throwing open his foot locker, Matthew discovered that the handheld VHF radio was also missing, but the folding .22 caliber rifle that he kept stored beneath the clothes at the bottom of the same container had remained untouched. He removed the gun and assembled it.

...

Completely incensed by his knowledge that Matthew had located the Thylacine den and kept it secret, Victor had gone directly to base camp and called the helicopter with the two-way radio. Once he was certain that the aircraft was on its way, he bashed the big radio repeatedly with a large rock so no one else could use it.

After locating the agreement papers, a spare hypodermic kit and the trammel net, he made himself a cup of tea and relaxed. Upon hearing the sound of the approaching helicopter, he had lugged the net and the rest of his gear out to the landing site and waited to be picked up.

Sam Strickland was not surprised to see a lone figure waiting for his arrival at base camp. What bewildered him was Michael's total astonishment when they landed at the lakeside camp in the Walls of Jerusalem basin.

"What's going on? Where's Matthew?" Michael inquired.

"I don't know and don't care. That bastard's

140

been holding out on us!" exclaimed Victor.

"What!?"

Both Michael and Strickland stood unbelieving and waited for an explanation.

"I became suspicious a few days ago, so I decided to follow him when he went back to base camp. Instead of going there, he made for a Thylacine den that he had already known about... who knows for how long? I'm not sure what he was planning but it obviously didn't include us."

"You saw this Thylacine den?" asked Michael incredulously.

"Better than that, I saw the animals themselves, two of them. Matthew had made himself a blind and was just sittin' there watching them. Here are his notes."

The men took the notebook and examined it. It was true.

"Where's Matthew now?" Strickland inquired.

"I challenged him and we got into a fight. I suppose he's still out there."

"What do you mean? Did you kill him?"

"No, but maybe I should have," said Victor. "I only knocked him out to keep him from hitting my face again."

The men examined Victor closely. He sported several bruises where Matthew had punched him.

"Damn!" exclaimed Michael. "I trusted him completely. What do you reckon we ought to do?"

"Go back there right now and catch those two

141

animals," replied Victor. "If Matthew tries to stop us, I'll knock him senseless and then tie him up this time."

"We had better get going," Strickland suggested, "and I hope the place is not too far - I've got to maintain enough fuel reserve to get back to the airport."

"It's practically on the way," Victor assured him.

With that comment, Michael abruptly abandoned everything.

"Let's get the hell out of here!" he cried.

...

It was difficult to find a landing spot for the helicopter near the den site. The closest they could do without wasting a lot of time and fuel was to set down a kilometre or so northeast of it in a place where the forest opened up some.

Once they had landed, all three men quickly marched over to the small stream that circled the rocky ridge and followed it to where the den was situated. As soon as they saw the spot, both Michael and Strickland knew that something dramatic had happened here. Matthew's gear was scattered around the dome tent. Inside, the remains of his first-aid kit indicated that he had doctored himself before leaving.

"I wonder where he went?" Strickland pondered.

"Who cares?" Victor answered. "He can take care of himself. Let's get those animals and get out of here."

"That must be the den," Michael said when he

saw the opening.

"I'll bet they're inside. Stick your head in and see if you can hear anything," Victor instructed.

Michael stuck his head in and leaned forward, listening carefully. Several small squeaking sounds and some scuffling noises drifted up to him.

"There's definitely something in there! Sounds like the whimpering of pups," he cried.

"Good. Let's set up the trammel net and we'll smoke them out. Once they get tangled in that net, we'll have 'em."

With their knives and a hatchet Victor had brought, the men removed the brush surrounding the den site. Then they cut eight two-metre-long poles from a clump of saplings growing near the creek. The poles were erected in a semicircle five metres in diameter around the den by setting them in a series of holes dug into the ground or by supporting them with small cairns made of rocks. The net was then draped loosely over each pole, creating a circular wall with one open end.

Victor entered the circle carrying a "smoke bomb" made from a bundle of dried grass. After lighting it, he tossed it down into the hole and quickly got away. Closing the circle of net, he positioned himself outside with the others and waited. It didn't take long. In less than minute, the big male streaked out of the den and crashed into the net at Michael's feet.

"I've got him, I've got him!" cried Michael.

"Don't let the top of the net collapse to the ground, there's more animals down there!" Victor

143

shouted.

Immediately, the female shot out of the hole and hit the net between Victor and Strickland.

"Fold the top of the net over them," Victor ordered. "Quickly now!"

In a few seconds, the men had trapped both terrified Thylacines in a layer of netting that securely held them. While Strickland and Michael kept the animals subdued with the weight of their bodies, Victor gave each an injection. The struggling soon stopped.

"Let's carry them over to the chopper and get them out of here," Victor ordered. "They'll be unconscious for at least three hours. If they start to wake up before we get to Hobart, I'll give them another shot."

"What about the pups?" Michael asked anxiously, while peering into the den's entrance again. The whimpering sounds were much louder now.

"If they don't come out in a couple of minutes, we'll have to leave them," said Victor. "They seemed like they might be big enough to take care of themselves."

For ten minutes, smoke continued to pour out of the hole but neither of the pups appeared.

"We can't wait any longer... let's get going," ordered Victor. "Better bring that net with us, Kid, we'll need it if these animals get loose somehow."

"Here, I'll carry it," offered Strickland.

The hike back to the helicopter did not take more than twenty minutes, even with the unconscious

144

weight of the thirty kilogram male draped over Victor's shoulders. Michael carried the smaller female, which weighed at least twenty kilos, in the same manner. He was so excited that he hardly noticed the load. Everyone was ecstatic, even Strickland. They would soon be receiving the big bonus that they had been working so long to get.

After laying both animals on the floor of the back seat, Victor climbed in next to them so he could handle things should they wake up. Michael rode up front, in the copilot's position. He was grinning from ear to ear when they lifted off the ground and began to rise above the forest. An hour and forty minutes later as they approached an airstrip south of Deloraine, Strickland indicated that he wanted a cloth shroud placed over the Thylacines.

"I've got friends here but we don't want anyone to start asking questions when we stop to refuel," he explained over the intercom. "Just let me handle the conversation."

"Suits me fine, mate," Michael replied, remembering to press the "talk" button.

The refueling went smoothly and soon the aircraft was following the Lake Highway south towards Hobart. Numerous silver lakes dotted the late afternoon scenery like blobs of mercury from a broken thermometer.

To Michael, the dark road that they were following gave the landscape a sense of direction and purpose. As he stared in fascination, he imagined that the automobiles traveling along the thin line below him were brightly colored ants hurriedly running from nest to nest. He wondered if real ants led such urgent lives. A voice in his intercom headset brought him sharply back to reality.

"Michael, we'll be in Hobart in less than an hour. It's only about two hundred kilometres from here," Strickland informed him.

Michael twisted around to look at Victor.

"One more hour!" he yelled above the machine's noise while pointing at his watch. Victor nodded and offered the "thumbs up" signal.

It was nearly dusk when Strickland approached the civilian airport outside of Hobart. He could see that the Learjet had already arrived and was waiting on the tarmac below, near a row of private hangers.

Calling the control tower, he requested clearance to land in the vicinity of the jet. He had some passengers to transfer, he explained.

"Helicopter five-three-three-foxtrot-tango, you are cleared for landing," came the reply over his radio.

Two men approached the helicopter as soon as it touched down and shut off its engine.

"You have some special cargo you want transferred?" one of the men asked.

"Two special cargoes," Victor replied. "Do you have a couple of cages ready to receive them?"

Both strangers nodded "yes."

"They are still knocked out from the drugs, so they will be fairly easy to handle," Victor continued. "It would probably be a good idea, though, to carry them wrapped up in the cloth. It would draw less attention from anyone passing by."

It was agreed and the transfer was completed in less than ten minutes. Although their precaution was entirely appropriate, no one had so much as driven by during the whole time. It was a quiet part of the airport.

Shaking hands with Strickland, Victor said, "Good work! There'll be a bonus in the mail for you when we get back from where we're going."

With a salute-like wave, Strickland turned and headed back to his helicopter, while one of the men from the Learjet pulled up the plane's loading steps and closed the door. A high-pitched whine indicated that pilot was starting its engines.

His helper quickly indicated that Victor and Michael should sit down until they were airborne, bid them to make themselves comfortable, and then went forward to join the pilot in the cockpit. His manner was efficient and impersonal.

The Thylacine cages were tied to the mounting rails that had once held the rear seats. Each contained a still-sleeping animal, gently held upright by "squeezing" the cage's interior space with a moveable wall that could be locked into any position.

Both Victor and Michael sat in the remaining two seats that had been remounted in reverse position in order to face the cages. The interior of a Learjet is surprisingly cramped but the men made the best of it. It was important that they were able to watch the cages throughout the whole trip and make sure the animals were comfortable when they woke up.

Ten minutes later, the jet was aloft and headed north. In less time than it took Michael to roll and smoke a cigarette, they had passed back over the expedition's base camp, streaking across the sky at more than eight-hundred-and-fifty kilometres per hour at an altitude of twenty-eight thousand feet.

After a while, the copilot came back out of the cockpit to join his passengers.

"So this is the special cargo that we installed these cages for?" he asked. "What sort of critters are they?"

"Thylacines," Victor replied.

"What?"

"Tasmanian tigers," Michael chimed in.

"Tasmanian tigers? I've heard of them... but aren't they supposed to be extinct?"

Victor and Michael looked at each other, a slow smile crept across their faces. When Michael turned back towards the copilot, he wore a look of immense satisfaction.

"Yes, they are," was his only reply.

"Interesting," the copilot murmured to himself. "Anyway, there's some food and drink in the box sitting on the jump seat behind the pilots' seats," he said, pointing. "The toilet's underneath the seat's cushion and you can pull this little curtain around you for privacy."

"Help yourself to anything you like. I've got to

get back to the cockpit and keep the captain awake. It will be almost midnight before we reach Cairns and sunrise when we get to where we're headed."

"Thanks," said Michael. "I had no idea that Learjets were so small inside. It's like riding in a big darning needle with wings."

"Yes, it is a bit cramped," smiled the copilot. "But this machine will get us where we're going... fast."

In Cairns, Victor and Michael were instructed to keep the cabin window shutters closed while the plane was being refueled. The first three hour leg of the journey had gone well and Victor had managed to even take a short nap.

As the effects of the drugs wore off, both Thylacines began to waken. To further restrain their occupants, Victor gently moved the "squeeze" handles towards the center of the cages. The male animal objected to this treatment, letting out a long "Yipe!" that was so loud that the men thought it might attract the notice of the ground attendants working around the outside of the aircraft. But no one seemed to notice or bothered to look inside of the plane.

Chapter Fifteen

After filing a flight plan to clear Australian airspace, the jet took off into the pre-dawn sky. At an altitude of twenty-nine thousand feet, they leveled off for cruising. The Thylacines had quieted down and the squeeze cages were slightly relaxed in order to make the animals more comfortable. The female groomed her forelegs and shoulders while the male simply laid on the bottom of his cage and watched everything that went on around him with evident curiosity.

Michael walked forward to the cockpit. "How ya going, mates? You mind if I watch for a while?" he asked.

"Not at all... glad to have the company," greeted the pilot. "However, I would advise you sit in the jump seat while you're up here. The air's liable to get a bit bumpy when we cross over New Guinea's mountains."

After an hour and a half of level flight, the pilot put the plane into steep descent.

"Are we there already?" asked Michael.

"No, not exactly... this is where we do some fancy flying," the copilot answered. "Hang on."

"Cairns Control, this is Learjet six-eight-seven-Papa-November-Charlie. I'm twenty-two miles out from Wewak, descending out of two-forty," the copilot spoke clearly into the microphone of his radio headset.

"Roger, Learjet six-eight-seven," came the reply over the speaker.

Michael's presence was forgotten as the two pilots now prepared for a false "landing." A few moments later the copilot spoke again to the air traffic controller.

"Cairns Control, this Learjet six-eight-seven-Papa-November-Charlie. We are less than two-thousand and have airport on visual, going to VFR, canceling my flight-plan."

"Roger, Learjet six-eight-seven. Your flight plan is terminated. Squawk twelve-hundred and contact advisory frequencies."

The air traffic controller had stopped tracking the Learjet and ordered it to change its transponder to twelve-hundred, an international frequency. The plane was now on its own.

Michael stared in fascination as the lights of the runway came into view and rushed quickly towards them. Instead of landing, though, the pilot roared over the field at full throttle and upon reaching the end of the runway pulled the controls back into a sharp climb. At the same time, the copilot switched off the transponder and calmly spoke into the radio.

"Cairns control, this is Learjet six-eight-seven-Papa-November-Charlie. We have landed. We have landed. Thank you for your assistance."

"Roger, Learjet six-eight-seven. Have a good visit. Cairns control out."

The jet plane leveled out at one thousand feet and reduced power to sixty-five percent throttle.

"Let's keep her at two-hundred and ten knots,"

the captain advised his copilot. "We're going to be burning a lot of fuel."

It was then that they noticed that Michael was still sitting in the jump seat, gripping the doorway with white-knuckled intensity. The plane bucked and jerked in the unstable air of the lower atmosphere.

"You okay?" the copilot asked.

"Yeah! I... I think so. Wow, what a rush! Where are we going now?"

"We're headed for a rendezvous on an island about two hundred nautical miles offshore from here. In order to maintain secrecy, we're flying at low altitude, below the radar detection zone. Air traffic control thinks that we've landed back at that little uncontrolled airport at Wewak, New Guinea, and below fifteen hundred feet, there's no radar to spot us."

"Trouble is," said the captain, "we use more than five times as much fuel flying at this low altitude than we would at thirty-thousand feet."

"We're not going have much fuel to spare on arrival... so, heaven help us if we get lost," the copilot added. "At our present rate of consumption, it looks like we have about an hour and thirty minutes to 'silence.'"

"Silence?"

"That's when the engines quit."

Heavy turbulence rocked the plane sharply, causing Michael to bump his head on the bulkhead.

"It might be best if you went back to your seat and buckle yourself in... we're entering a rain squall."

Michael had barely gotten seated when the turbulence resumed in earnest. Victor did not seem to be enjoying the ride either and had turned slightly green. He reached for an airsickness bag in the pocket behind the seat.

A lightning flash illuminated the entire row of starboard windows. The pilots changed their course, trying to fly around the worst part of the storm... the large thunderhead that their radar indicated was looming in front of them. Another lightning flash briefly lit the plane's interior. Michael noticed that his palms were moist with sweat.

Then it was over. Suddenly, the ride became so smooth, that for a moment Michael thought the engines had indeed "silenced." He could still feel their vibration through the seat, though. They had passed through the rough spot. The Thylacines had remain calm throughout the plane's wild maneuvering.

Michael unfastened his seat belt and again made his way back up to the cockpit, this time much more warily. However, as soon as the copilot saw him, he suggested that he return to his seat.

"We seem to have wandered off course a bit, mate," the copilot advised him. "But we'll be getting back on track soon. Now that we're getting some daylight, we ought to be able to see our island pretty quick."

Michael returned to his seat and remained quiet. Victor still was looking a bit ill.

"You okay, Victor?"

"I never was a great flyer, Kid... especially when it becomes bumpy. But I'm okay. This bouncing around has just unsettled my stomach a bit." He picked up the barf bag and retched into it again.

"This is the first weak point I've seen in Victor," Michael muttered to himself as he closed his eyes and leaned back into his seat. "He's just like the rest of us."

It seemed like an eternity before they heard the wing flaps lower and the landing gear lock into place. There was another long disturbing pause, then a sharp bump... touchdown and the braking of forward momentum. They had arrived at the rendezvous point.

When the exit door opened, it revealed a nearly flat island landscape relieved only by a few dunes of glaring white sand in the distance, fronted by a line of heavily-limbed trees above the beach. Most of the island's interior was covered with short heath-like shrubs that swayed and dipped in the breeze. The airstrip, composed of hard-packed crushed rock, seemed to be in excellent repair, especially since it dated back to World War II.

A hundred feet away from the Learjet stood a much larger jet airplane, its nose facing the morning sun. Victor was the first to deplane.

"All right! It's nice be on solid ground again," he exclaimed. He was his old self again.

Michael and the two pilots joined him and they walked in a group towards the other plane.

Two men stepped out of the large plane and moved to either side of the stairway. By the attentive manner of their stance, Victor instantly recognized them as bodyguards.

"Looks like the 'Boss' is coming out now," Victor commented without turning his head to look at Michael.

Yeoh Chin Choo stepped lightly from the plane into the glare of the morning sun. Two more men followed him. One carried a briefcase, the other cradled an Uzi submachine gun across his chest. The sight of the gun caused Michael's step to falter. He glanced nervously towards Victor, who walked calmly forward. Michael stayed close to his side.

"Good morning gentlemen!" Chin greeted the men. "I'm Yeoh Chin Choo. Is Mr. Clark still in the plane?"

"No, I'm afraid he declined to accompany us on this trip," replied Victor.

"Is he all right?"

"He's as well as can be expected under the circumstances. He met a bit of trouble recently."

"Oh, I see." Chin was very perceptive and immediately realized that Victor had taken over Matthew's place.

"Do you understand the terms of the agreement, Mr...?"

"Victor... Victor Siegle. This is my junior associate Michael Strezelecki. He's a fine tracker... one of the best. Yes, I understand the situation."

Handshakes followed the introduction.

"G'day, sir," Michael beamed.

"How is the 'product' doing? Let's have a look at it," said Chin, while indicating with a wave of his hand that the group should move over to the Learjet.

"There's two of them, Mr. Choo," Victor informed him.

Chin smiled slightly and then corrected Victor. "It's Mr. Yeoh. Unlike you Westerners, we Chinese place our family names first. My name is Mr. Yeoh."

"Excuse me, sir. I didn't know," Victor replied apologetically. He wondered if Chin had heard him mention that there was more than one animal.

Chin paused at the foot of the stairway while the man with the briefcase went up and entered the plane, presumably to inspect the cargo. The man with the Uzi stood behind Victor and Michael. After a moment, a head appeared in the doorway and spoke to Chin in clipped Mandarin Chinese.

"Would you mind helping us move the cages over to my plane before we conclude this transaction?" Chin asked.

"Not at all, Mr. Yeoh," replied Victor, fully aware that he was in no position to bargain.

Michael was amazed at the luxuriant interior of Chin's plane. There were four overstuffed leather-covered seats, one facing the other, separated by a polished wood table on each side of the aircraft. Two uniformed pilots sat at one of the tables drinking coffee. At the rear of the plane was a rest room, complete with wash basin and toilet.

The pilots rose to help with the cages, installing

them just behind the bulkhead separating the main cabin from the entry. They were fastened into the floor tracks that had previously secured the two seats that been removed.

"Please have a seat, gentlemen, and we'll conclude our business," invited Chin after Victor and Michael and the two pilots had finished the task. He gently motioned for the armed guard to remain outside.

"I think we'll go for a walk," one of the Learjet pilots said as they de-boarded the plane. "Perhaps we can start refueling for the return trip?"

"My pilots can help you," Chin offered.

"Would you care for some coffee?" asked Chin courteously when he turned back to the table.

"Yes, that would be nice. Please make mine black," replied Victor.

"Do you have cream and sugar?" asked Michael.

The man with the briefcase left his seat and went to the small galley cabinet in the forward part of the main cabin to prepare the drinks.

While they were waiting, Chin went over to the Thylacine cages and looked at the animals. Victor and Michael related all they knew about the animals' care to Chin and then to the man who returned with the coffee. It turned out that their "waiter" was actually a veterinarian.

"I've never seen such a plane before," remarked Michael as he gazed about. "What kind is it?"

"This one was built in America. It's called a

Cessna Citation. It's capable of flying nonstop for more than three-thousand-five-hundred miles and can reach a top speed of nearly six hundred miles per hour, almost the speed of sound."

"Wow! That's amazing."

Chin smiled tolerantly, then reached over and picked up the briefcase. Opening it, he revealed fourteen four-inch high bundles of one-hundred dollar bills arranged in two rows.

"There's a million dollars in here, gentlemen. Half of it is in Australian currency and the other half in U.S. funds. I hope that is acceptable to you?"

"Yes, it is," replied Victor. "But it was our understanding that we were to be paid five million dollars for two of these animals."

"Of course...of course. This is just the cash portion of my payment. There are also eight certified bank drafts for five-hundred thousand dollars each, issued by OCBC, the biggest banking corporation in all of Asia. Please look them over if you will... you can deposit them in any bank in the world. We normally don't carry any cash for our business transactions. It's terribly bulky and hard to manage. This little bit is just some 'pocket money' that Mr. Clark had requested."

"Look's good to me, Mr. Yeoh," said Victor. "Let's consider the transaction complete. Shall we shake on it?"

The three men stood and shook hands all around.

"Well, I guess these animals are in good hands.

So long and thanks."

Victor and Michael departed the big jet, leaving Chin and the veterinarian to discuss the animals' care.

"We're rich!" Michael exclaimed.

"Yep! That we are," said Victor. "I sure could use a good breakfast. Seems like forever since I've had a decent meal."

"I'm too excited to think about food."

"Well, let's see if we can lend our pilots a hand. The sooner we get out of here the better I'll feel."

There were over twenty drums of jet fuel cached in a crude shelter at the end of the runway near the two planes. Each fifty-gallon drum had to be rolled out to the plane where it was stood upright and fitted with a hand pump and transfer hose.

Since eight strokes of the pump handle moved only one gallon of fuel, the process was slow and tedious, especially under the growing heat of the tropical sun. Even with taking turns working the pump handle, it took nearly three hours and twelve barrels of fuel to refill the Learjet.

"You guys want a hand putting the rest of this fuel in your plane?" Victor asked one of Chin's pilots. He knew that they both could speak English.

"Thanks, we could always use a good topping off," he replied.

By two o'clock in the afternoon, both planes were ready for departure. Chin had not made a reappearance since the conclusion of the deal.

With a parting salute, the Learjet pilots

positioned for takeoff, warmed and revved its engines, and released the brakes. The plane shot down the runway. It was very close to the far end when, abruptly, it lifted off the ground and began a steep skyward ascent. As they banked in a slow southward turn towards Australia, Victor and Michael peered down and saw that the other plane was just beginning its roll down the runway.

"Where do you guys want to be let off?" asked the copilot when they had reached cruising altitude.

"How about Sydney?" replied Victor. "Is that all right with you, Kid?"

"Sure!"

"How much do we owe you guys?" asked Victor.

"Not a thing, mate. This ride is part of the deal."

"Michael, what do you say we give these guys a bonus?" continued Victor as he opened the briefcase.

"Fine by me."

"Well then, why don't you give them a couple of these bundles?"

"What's your preference? Yank or Aussie dollars?" asked Michael laughing.

Chapter Sixteen

Matthew had hardly noticed the thin contrail created by the northbound jet carrying Victor, Michael, and the Thylacines as they passed overhead on their way to meet Yeoh Chin Choo. At that moment he was busy folding a blanket and filling his day pack with some of the camp's scattered food supplies in preparation to going back to the den site.

His swollen eye and his head throbbed with pain. Weak from exhaustion and unable to walk properly, he should have been getting some needed rest. But he was determined to get there as soon as possible. He arrived on the afternoon of the following day.

Matthew's tent was still standing where he had left it but his belongings were widely strewn about. Several of the bushes around the den's entrance had been hacked away, and a ring of telltale poles left mute evidence that the trammel net had been employed.

He stuck his head into the entrance and listened carefully; a faint whining sound seeped from deep within. Something was still inside. Hoping that Victor and Michael had been unable to catch the animals, he went back into the blind, made himself as comfortable as possible, and watched.

If the adult animals had been scared away before they were trapped, he speculated, then it was possible that they may return for the pups. It was even conceivable that they were inside the den at that moment, waiting for the cover of darkness before going out.

Huddling inside the tent, with his rifle at his side, Matthew stared at the den with his one good eye as the evening light faded into darkness. As tired as he was, he was able to force himself to stay awake until long after midnight. Finally, he slumped over onto the tent floor and slept a deep dreamless sleep. No animal had made an appearance.

When the harsh reality of daylight brought consciousness back to him, it was already midmorning. He ate a quick breakfast of tinned fruit and then went over to examine the soil in front of the den. It had not been disturbed... nothing had come out or gone in since his arrival. Something was terribly wrong.

Sticking his head into the entrance again, he listened for nearly five minutes before he heard the faint whimper. By angling the light from his electric torch over his head and squeezing into the hole as far as possible, he could just see part of a small furry body lying on its side, breathing heavily. It was one of the pups and it looked like it was dying. Remnants of burnt grass lay around it. Matthew now understood; the adult Thylacines had been smoked out.

Frantically, he tried to enlarge the den's entrance so that he could squeeze in further and rescue the pup, but the solid rock was unforgiving. Failing that, he tried poking the little animal with a stick but it was too weak to even respond. While he watched in horror, its little chest gave a final heave and then it lay still. The pup was dead.

Breaking into tears, Matthew tried desperately to slide its small body towards the entrance with his stick. At one point he could almost reach a foreleg with his outstretched hand, but the corpse suddenly rolled away and out of sight.

Completely frustrated, he backed out of the hole and screamed with rage. A flock of Green rosellas were startled up into the tree canopy, then all was quiet again. A giddy dizziness seemed to overwhelm Matthew, forcing him to laugh crazily, like a madman. For a long while he sat in the center of this desolate scene, with his camping equipment strewn about and the Thylacine den staring like a burned out eye, alternately laughing and raging to the sky. At length, he pulled himself to his feet, returned to the tent, picked up his rifle, grabbed some necessary gear, and left.

Without a radio, he could not call for help. He would have to walk out to the nearest road, at least four days away. In his present condition, Matthew seriously doubted he could do the trip in less than a week, if at all. Until he felt better, it would be best to return to base camp and rest.

Two days later, the swelling around his eye subsided enough to allow him to see again, though the tissue around the area remained a violent shade of purple. Even though he still limped, he was becoming extremely restless and before midmorning, he abandoned base-camp.

With no accurate topo map to follow, it was

likely to be a long and arduous trek. Matthew's best hope was to hike southwest through the temperate rainforest filled with leatherwood, myrtle, and huge tree-ferns to the headwaters of the Nive River, then follow this waterway downstream until he eventually encountered a road.

Not surprisingly, his limp did not improve throughout the entire ordeal. The terrain was so difficult that he often fell flat on his face, straight into the ever-present mud or onto bruising rocks. However, there was occasional relief from this misery; whenever he laid down to rest, he blacked out from fatigue as quickly as if someone had hit him with a baseball bat.

For one full day he was lost - trapped really - in a large expanse of horizontal scrub. Worse than a nightmare, this misery was caused by a slender beech tree, a thicket-forming species found only in this region, whose main stems angle off sideways after attaining just a few feet of vertical growth. The resulting lattice of limbs not only makes bushwalking difficult but bloody dangerous. More than once Matthew fell completely through the network of interlocking branches to the ground. Each time, he had to muster all his reserves of patience and energy before he could extricate himself. He could not imagine Hell being a worse place to fall into.

Matthew's constant southwestern course of travel blindly led him to a chain of small clear lakes linked by a tiny fern-choked stream. According to his sketchy map, this waterway flowed southward to the mainstream of the Nive River. Desperately hoping that the map was not wrong, he floundered across moss-covered logs and around algae-coated boulders until a much larger stream blocked his passage. He had reached the Nive at last!

The Nive River is a steep rocky slash in the dark green forest, filled at the moment to overflowing with a foaming torrent of water. Most of the time it was too dangerous to travel alongside the river itself. Usually Matthew had to retreat part-way up the slippery, vine-and-tree-choked slope of the steep valley cut through by the river.

At last, he was forced to climb to the top of the first terrace and there, literally stumbled onto a logging road. A stroke of good luck. Within an hour of following its winding track, Matthew came to the main road and soon hitchhiked a ride in a truck to the roadhouse at Bronte. Like most roadhouses in Tasmania, this one was a combination cafeteria, petrol-stop, and motel.

The simple meal, shower, and bed that this facility provided that night seemed absolutely luxurious. Especially the shower... to Matthew's way of thinking, a hot shower was the best thing that civilization had to offer.

"If you don't agree," he was quick to say, "try taking one after a month of denial or a couple weeks of slogging through the waterlogged forests of Tasmania."

After more than fourteen hours of sleep, Matthew awoke just in time to catch the daily bus to

Hobart. From the bus station, it was just a short taxi ride to the quiet neighborhood where his house stood. The spare key was still hidden under the flat rock in the flower garden next to the steps.

...

Matthew's son, Brian, had been collecting his mail from the postbox and gathering up the newspapers from the front steps. He even had mowed the lawn once or twice to keep his father from being fined by the local neighborhood improvement committee. His house-keeping efforts, however, were not so commendable. He hadn't even washed the dirty dishes that Matthew had left behind several months ago.

In a frenzy of hot water and concentrated dish soap, Matthew finally cleaned up the kitchen and then retired with a beer in hand to the sofa, in order to sort through and read some of the more recent newspapers and letters. One paper bore the headline: "Tasmanian Tigers Alive." Another screamed, "Extinct Thylacines Smuggled Out of Country!" Apparently, Victor and Michael had been successful with their rendezvous with Chin.

The news was even on television. Later that night, Matthew watched a locally produced documentary about Thylacines. From this program, he learned that both adult animals had been captured and were on display in a specially-built glass cage in the luxurious Yellow Dragon Hotel in Taiwan. There were shots of a proud Yeoh Chin Choo making special announcements to the press, close-ups of the Thylacines in their bulletproof cage, talk about 24-hour guards and an electronic security system, and scenes of a curious and excited crowd. The human zoo.

The news concerning the Thylacines was not all favorable, though. There was a growing public outcry about trapping and holding these animals in captivity. The World Wildlife Fund and other wildlife conservation groups were putting political pressure on Taiwan to sign the CITES Treaty and return the Tasmanian tigers to their homeland. Chin appeared again, this time on late night news, flanked by Taiwanese government officials, saying that if it hadn't been for his efforts, the world would have never known that Thylacines still existed. He said that he was doing the world a favor by putting these animals on display.

Ever hungry for a good story, the news media was giving this one a run for its money. The local program that Matthew had watched hinted at far-reaching concern by airing opinionated sound-bites from the United States, Japan, France, and even China. Somehow, these two animals - possibly the last survivors of their race - had caught the public's imagination and were becoming a symbol for the survival of the underdog.

For good or bad, the networks were trying to make the most of this latest craze. One call-in ad even offered a free Thylacine lapel pin for every $25 donation to its "free-the-captive-animals" fund.

169

Chapter Seventeen

Upset by all of these tidings, Matthew went to bed and lay in the dark with his hands behind his head. After two hours of staring at the ceiling, he still was not sleepy. Yeoh Chin Choo was obviously capitalizing on the surge of interest in his captives. Victor and Michael probably had split the "fee" and were living high on the hog somewhere.

"Perhaps I should try to get my share of the loot and then forget the whole thing," Matthew mused.

A motorcycle rumbling up the driveway at nearly half past one-o'clock in the morning jolted him back to the present.

"Brian?"

"Hi Dad! I didn't realize that you had gotten back," he said while opening a stubby bottle of beer and tossing the rest of the six-pack into the refrigerator. "You okay? You don't look so good. What happened to your eye?"

Without waiting for an answer, Brian brushed past Matthew and flopped down on the sofa. Placing his black leather boots up on the coffee table, he took a long pull on the bottle and then looked up at his father.

"My girl friend has locked me out," Brian stated. "It's over for sure. She won't even let me in long enough to get my stuff. I've been crashing here for the last couple of days."

"I haven't been doing so well, either," Matthew

admitted. "Wanna shout me a couple of those beers?"

...

Matthew didn't know how long he had been asleep when the ringing of the telephone woke him. There was plenty of sunlight outside, but he had no idea what time of day it was.

"H...Hello?"

"Hello, is this Mr. Clark?"

"Mmmmmm....."

"Mr. Clark, I'm Gerry Pederman with the *National Review*. I wonder if I could talk to you about the capture of the two Tasmanian tigers that you sold to Taiwan?"

"What?! I never... I mean, I don't know what you are talking about! Good-bye!"

Matthew hung up the receiver, sighed, and rolled over to go back to sleep. Unfortunately, a vague sense of worry had replaced whatever slumber was left in him. Still, he must have lain there for more than an hour before a sharp knock on the front door brought him to his feet. Two police officers greeted Matthew as he opened the door.

"Are you Matthew Clark?"

"Yes... What is the problem Officer?"

"I am Sergeant Joseph O'Neil and this is Corporal Jesse Hughes."

"<u>Yes</u>?"

"Sir, we have a warrant for your immediate arrest. You are charged with trafficking state and

172

federally protected wildlife. I must caution you that although you don't have to answer any further questions, any answers you do give may be taken down and used in evidence. Do you understand?"

Matthew nodded that he did and asked if he could get dressed before he went. He was still in his nightclothes.

"We'll accompany you to your room, sir. We will fetch your clothes and then hand them to you."

"My bedroom is at the end of the hall past the washroom."

"Are these yours?" the sergeant asked, lifting Matthew's trousers and shirt from the chair where he had carelessly tossed them.

"Yes, they are."

After checking the clothes for possible hidden weapons, the officer handed them to him.

"Are these your shoes?" he asked, pointing to his pair of worn running shoes.

Brian, who had just come in the house from working on his motorcycle out in the back yard, peered through the bedroom doorway as Matthew began to dress.

"What's going on Dad?"

"It looks like I'm being arrested, mate."

"What the hell for?!" he gasped.

"I'm being blamed for capturing those Thylacines that the media is making such a fuss about."

"Oh, Jesus!"

"Excuse me..." one of the policemen

173

interrupted. "Now that you've gotten dressed, please place your hands behind your back."

When Matthew did so, he snapped handcuffs over both wrists.

"There's no need to put Goddamn handcuffs on him!" Brian shouted. "What are you going to do, beat the shit out of him when you get him in the car?" Brian was getting extremely upset.

"Calm down, Kid, we're not going to hurt your old man... Let's go, sir."

As the police led Matthew down the walkway towards the car, he glanced back over his shoulder to where Brian stood on the doorstep. He was pale with shock.

"Don't worry Dad, I'll help you straighten this out."

...

Matthew spent the rest of the day and that night in jail before his solicitor managed to get him released on bail. As he waited for Brian to meet him with a car, Matthew overheard two bailiffs discussing his case as they walked passed. One mentioned that he thought the charges would probably be dropped after the media turned its attention elsewhere.

Upon hearing the conversation, Matthew's lawyer shrugged his shoulders and said, "I'll see what I can do. It does looks hopeful. After all, Thylacines are supposed to be extinct."

Just then Brian came through the heavy front

doors. He still looked upset.

"You okay, Dad?"

"Anhhh...no worries, mate."

"Dad, I have to confess, I was totally astounded to come into the house and find that you were being arrested. They treat you well while you were here?"

"As well as can be expected, son... at least they were polite to me through the whole thing."

"Yeah! You never know any more, what with all the beatings and crap that we see on the telly," Brian added reflectively.

"Hey look, Dad! You're on the front page," he blurted while shoving the local morning newspaper into his father's hands.

There it was for all to see: the story of Matthew's arrest. The reporter who called him yesterday had tipped off the police. Apparently one of the state ministers had become very upset when he began to be deluged with irate demands from representatives of the Green Party. The arrest warrant had been issued just two days after Yeoh Chin Choo's announcement that the Thylacines were on display in his hotel.

Brian stopped the car at a news agent to pick up a copy of the *National Review*. There it was again, on page one. The writer was the same person who had called Matthew on the telephone. He felt for "humanity's sake" that they should make an example of him. Not just a fine, but a prison term too, was his suggestion of the most fitting punishment.

175

After reading the rest of the article, things didn't look so good. Matthew desperately hoped that the charges would indeed be dropped when this affair became "old news."

All hope died, however, when the car neared Matthew's house. A small crowd of protesters was waiting to meet them.

"What are you going to do with all that money?" one indignant woman demanded.

"He's going to need it to keep out of jail," another chimed in.

"Let me through," Matthew said, forcing his way past the knot of people. He and Brian went into the house and locked the door behind them.

One by one, the demonstrators lost interest and drifted away. By evening, the street was clear.

"I hope that's the last of that," Matthew sighed.

Later in the night, Brian went out the back door for some take-away food. While waiting for his return, Matthew sat despondently at his desk and stared at a row of insect specimens that he had mounted years ago, long before this business with Thylacines had begun.

At last, Brian came in with some pizza and beer. He was bleeding from a cut on his eyebrow.

"What happened!?"

"Oh nothin'. Some blokes gave me some shit. So I gave some back."

"Was it about me?"

"Yeah, 'fraid so, Dad. But don't worry, I'm with you all the way," he assured his father. "Come on into the living room and we'll polish off this pizza."

The telephone rang before they had finished eating.

"I'll get it, Dad."

Matthew was expecting more bad news or harassment, but Brian called out, "It's a woman, she's friendly and she wants to meet with you."

"Who is it?" Matthew asked warily.

"She says her name is Patricia Kincaid."

Matthew's heart sank, "What does <u>she</u> want?"

"Shall I tell her that you're busy?"

"Yeh! Tell her that I've gone out."

"She says that she would like to get together for dinner and drinks. She's buying."

"Huh? ... Oh, what the heck," Matthew said in a resigned tone while reaching for the telephone.

"Hullo?"

"Mr. Clark?"

"Yes."

"This is..."

"Ms. Kincaid... My son told me. Why are you calling? Want to get your licks in along with everyone else?"

"No, Mr. Clark. I was totally surprised to hear that the Thylacines actually did exist. I want to learn more about them. I owe you an apology... will you meet me for dinner? Please?"

"Dinner? Since you put it that way, how can I refuse?" Matthew answered, glancing over at Brian. He was holding his hand in a thumbs-up position.

"Go ahead, Dad. I'll hold down the fort."

Popping a beer, Brian leaned back on the sofa. Matthew noticed, however, that he no longer placed his feet up on the table.

...

Matthew and Patricia Kincaid had agreed to meet at Povalov's, a popular Greek restaurant on the other side of town near the hotel district. Ms. Kincaid was already waiting at a secluded table when he arrived. She seemed much friendlier and more demure than when they had met at his camp several months ago. Perhaps the lighting of the restaurant had created just a momentary illusion, for she got right down to business as soon as he had seated himself.

"I don't know how much you were paid to smuggle those Tasmanian tigers, out of the country," she began, "and frankly, I don't care to know. Just tell me how you found them."

Matthew began to relate the story of what had happened since that morning when she left the base camp. As he talked about photos and tracks and the discovery of the den, through dinner and two glasses of wine, her gaze became more attentive. It was nearly closing time when he finished. Somehow, her manner seemed very sympathetic. Perhaps it was the wine.

"It's terrible that the two pups should have died like that. It makes me angry that those men could have been so heartless," she said, then adding, "Yet, I'm glad that you decided to study the Thylacines instead of

178

capturing them."

"It was only for a few days, then I would have led the capture, myself," Matthew insisted.

"I'm not so sure of that, Mr. Clark."

To be honest, at this point Matthew wasn't so sure either. This was the first time that he had related the whole story to anyone. In doing so, he had reviewed it for himself. He had not wished to hurt the Thylacines and would have been reluctant to aid in their capture. Living wild and free was much preferable to prison.

They left the restaurant and shouldered into the chilly breeze that always sweeps Hobart in the early hours of morning.

"Here's your car, Ms. Kincaid. Thanks for a lovely evening." Matthew held out his hand to her. She took it and held it softly.

"Patricia, please call me Patricia," she murmured, letting her hand remain in his.

"How much longer will you be staying in Tasmania?" Matthew inquired.

"Two more weeks, then it's back to the States for a while," she replied.

Matthew's heart was racing, but he felt awkward.

Was she setting a trap? I had better be careful.

He pulled his hand away and held the car door after she had unlocked it. Their eyes met again and Matthew wanted to take her into his arms, but he resisted the temptation.

"So long, Patricia. Thanks for listening to my side of the story."

...

It was long past daybreak by the time Matthew returned home. A car with several people in it blocked his driveway. As Matthew approached, they got out and faced him. The protesters were back; two of the women he recognized from yesterday. Apparently, they had brought along their boyfriends this time. Matthew was feeling embattled again.

"Do you mind letting me get up my driveway?" Matthew asked them through his open window. "You're trespassing, you know."

"Whatta you going to do about it?" one of the men retorted.

Matthew looked at him as he stood outside the door of his vehicle and pondered the question. He wore a leather jacket adorned with a short chain, faded blue jeans, heavy black boots also decorated with chains, and his head was shaved. Not a friendly looking sort. With his friends behind him, he was grinning defiance. Matthew had to do something. But what?

He decided to try to be reasonable and got out to talk to them.

"I know you've seen a lot of stuff about me in the news," he began, "but the whole thing is just a big misunderstanding."

"Yeh? And what did you do with all the money?" the surly one demanded. His breath reeked with alcohol.

"And I suppose those two caged animals in Taiwan are just a figment of our imagination, too!" one of the women jeered adamantly.

"I suppose he'd sell 'is own Mum," the other woman chimed in.

"Well, we won't let 'em have the chance!" the troublesome one announced. With that, he shoved Matthew against the side of the vehicle.

Matthew shoved back, and the man exaggeratedly fell to the ground, knocking over one of the women as he went.

"Ow!...ow!...ow!" she wailed.

"I didn't mean to hurt you," Matthew said, trying to comfort her.

"The 'ell you didn't," retorted the sullen one as he clamored back to his feet. "I have a mind to belt you one!"

Matthew easily ducked his swipe but he didn't expect to be hit from behind by the woman who had been knocked down. It felt like a brick had collided with his skull and then suddenly the lights went out.

Brian found him, stretched out on the grass, with the car still parked with its engine running.

"Dad! Dad! You okay?"

When Matthew opened his eyes, Brian's crouching figure was silhouetted against the sun. He could feel a warm trickle moving down his scalp.

"Dad! Are you okay? I didn't see what happened. I was sleeping in. I'm sorry!"

"It's not your fault, mate. However, it might be a good idea if you would drive me to a hospital."

"Sure, Dad."

As Brian helped Matthew to his feet, a flash went off in his face.

"What the hell?"

"It looks like some sort of reporter with a camera is here. Shall I run him off?"

"Thanks, son."

It actually could have been a brick that the woman hit Matthew with. There was a bruise on his head the size of a goose egg, and an inch-long gash in his scalp that required several stitches to close. The hospital wanted to keep him overnight for observation, just in case there was a concussion. Matthew insisted that he felt well enough to decline the offer, however, and soon left for home.

This time there were no protesters or reporters there to greet them when they went up the drive.

"I'll kick the livin' shit out of the whole lot, if they come around again!" Brian muttered. Fortunately for both of them, no one did.

...

The doctor advised Matthew to get plenty of rest and do nothing strenuous for the next three or four days. The dressing on his scalp was changed daily and showed no sign of infection. However, for the first couple of nights he developed a severe headache that prevented him from sleeping. Brian helped out by

182

doing most of the household chores. It was good to see him being so responsible.

After nearly a week of idleness Matthew was feeling much better. The doctor was also pleased with his progress. Actually, he was becoming very restless to do something. Anything. Then Patricia Kincaid showed up unexpectedly at the door one evening.

"I thought you were heading back to the States soon," Matthew blurted in surprise.

"I'm not supposed to leave for another three days," she explained. "May I come in?"

"Oh! Certainly. Jeeze... where are my manners? You caught me at an unexpected moment. Would you care for a beer?"

"A cup of coffee would be nice, if you don't mind."

"Not at all, Ms. Kincaid."

"Patricia."

"Yes... Patricia," he repeated. "What brings you here? It's good to see you again." Her smile was open and friendly. He was struck again by how attractive she was.

"I read in the paper about that attack out in your driveway. I'm sorry... are you all right?"

"I'm getting better every day," he said, smiling wistfully. "The sitting and waiting is beginning to wear on me a bit, though."

"Oh yes! Your upcoming trial," she remembered. "Do you think they will go through with it?"

"My lawyer says that there's a good chance that they won't - that they're just letting me sweat for a while until the press turns the heat off."

"Yes, that makes good political sense," she said, summing up Matthew's situation with a very professional attitude. After a moment's pause, she added, "How would you like to do something about it?"

"What do you mean?"

"What if were possible to 'recapture' the Thylacines and bring them back to the Tasmanian wilderness for release?"

"What?! Are you serious?" Matthew had started to say "crazy" but checked himself. "That's impossible!"

"Is it, Mr. Clark?... Is it really?"

"I can't see how in the world..."

"Please, hear me out... then call me crazy if you want to."

He listened to the idea. It was a bold unformulated plan, involving some mates of Patricia's, mates who were willing to help with active participation and money. She was even ready to use her own savings to help make it work.

As she talked, the audaciousness of the idea actually began to appeal to Matthew. Could it be possible to truly pull something like this off? Somehow, he began to suspect that there was more than mere suggestion behind Patricia's proposal and that she had rehearsed what she was telling him.

"I would like to bring some people by tomorrow

184

evening so you can hear more about this from them."

Intrigued by the idea's novelty, Matthew agreed.

"See you around half past six?" she asked happily. "That's tea-time, isn't it? Maybe I'll bring a little snack along to go with your beer."

With that she backed out through the door and left. Matthew sprang forward to escort her to her car, but she waved him off.

"No need to bother, Mr. Clark, I can take care of myself."

He was to soon learn, that Patricia Kincaid could, indeed, take care of herself.

...

Three carloads of people showed up for the meeting. Patricia had exceeded Matthew's expectations with her organizational skills and influence. Besides Patricia, there were four men and another woman, much younger than her. All of them seemed to be brimming with purposefulness. Patricia's "snack" turned out to be an entire buffet that literally covered the table when it was unpacked from its boxes. Each person, in turn, introduced him or herself. One man, named Shawn Martin, Matthew recognized as a subordinate clerk at the local Parks and Wildlife Department. This was a bit of a surprise. The younger woman, Katrina, was his girlfriend. They firmly believed that "this was the right thing to do" and were eager for the adventure.

There was also Bill Schwartz, an outdoor-loving

middle-aged attorney who had kept in good physical shape; Troy Norris, a big cruiser and yacht captain by profession and idealist in temperament; and Robert Tan, a Chinese immigrant from Hong Kong who had moved his computer business to Melbourne ten years ago. Because he spoke fluent Mandarin and Cantonese, Robert's help would be critical when they arrived in Taipei.

As diverse as their backgrounds were, this collection of unlikely adventurers shared a common aspiration sprung from an ethic deeply imbedded in the Australian psyche. As a whole, Australians are fiercely protective of their wildlife, especially when they are in trouble. Recently, thousands of school children had donated a week's worth of their lunch money in support of research to help Koalas when a mysterious eye disease threatened an entire population of these loveable animals.

Australians also show great respect and support for the iconic "battler" - the person who trudges on against all odds. This includes the underdog or anyone who appears to be getting a raw deal. Shawn and his girl-friend, Bill, Troy, Robert, and Patricia - brought together by these and perhaps other more personal reasons - now sat in Matthew's house and discussed the "idea."

Over plates of food washed down with great quantities of beer, they excitedly began to formulate a rudimentary plan of action. The meeting was becoming rather lively when Brian rolled up on his motorcycle and came into the house.

"G'day son, have a beer and join us," Matthew called when he appeared in the doorway. Brian's surprised look slowly spread into a broad grin.

"Don't mind if I do, Dad. This is more like it... it's been like a tomb around here lately. What's this all about?"

Matthew introduced him to the group and he immediately fell in with the young couple, who began talking excitedly with him.

Sometime during the evening - perhaps around midnight - the gathering coalesced into a serious business meeting. By then, Matthew had begun to believe that the idea to recapture the Thylacines and bring them back to Tasmania actually had merit. He was glowing from good food, conversation, and beer.

"Okay," Matthew acknowledged, "We're going to need a good chunk of money in order to make this work."

Patricia laid a wad of traveler's checks on the coffee table. "There's seven thousand dollars in U.S. funds here and I can transfer another two or three thousand over here by wire tomorrow."

The young couple laid down three thousand and four-hundred in fifty-dollar bills.

"This is all we have, but I hope it helps," Katrina added. Matthew suspected that this probably represented a serious financial strain to them.

Troy kicked in fifteen thousand, Robert Tan wrote a check for twenty-eight thousand eight-hundred and Bill Schwartz, not having either ready cash or a checkbook on him at the moment, wrote "$60,000" on a slip of paper and laid it on top of the pile.

"That is my promissory note," he explained. "With nearly one-hundred and fifteen thousand dollars in the pot, I guess we'll be able to do <u>something</u>."

Matthew was impressed. "Well, if we're going to be throwing our money away, I have nearly twenty-five thousand dollars left over from the expedition," he said expansively while writing the figures on a scrap of paper and tossing it into the pile. "I guess I'm in."

The monetary commitment proved even more heady than the beer and wine they were drinking and their excitement grew tremendously. As they pondered the plan, they discussed each aspect in minute detail. Patricia quietly kept notes, while Brian watched the proceedings with wide-eyed interest.

After hours of planning, they seemed to have reached a consensus on how to proceed. First of all, they would not carry weapons of any kind and would try and avoid any situation where gunplay might occur. They also agreed that they needed one more person on the team: someone to pilot a rented helicopter that they would use for escape. Finally, at three o'clock in the morning, the meeting began to break up.

"Don't bother cleaning up, I can get to it in the morning," Matthew insisted as everyone except Patricia and Brian gathered near the door in preparation to leaving. Patricia stopped Matthew with a shake of her head when he tried to protest her carrying a load of dishes into the kitchen. The rest of the group laughed and headed for their vehicles.

"Care for a cup of coffee?" she asked from the kitchen.

Seized by a mysterious urgency, Brian also announced his departure and a moment later the deep-throated sound of his motorcycle roared down the driveway. Matthew had shrugged his move off at the time, but later he learned that Brian had left in order to be alone and deal with a personal problem that had been bothering him for a long time.

In the cold pre-dawn he had zipped across the long Tasman Bridge and didn't stop until daybreak found him at the beach near Primrose Point. Walking to the water's edge, he threw rocks at waves until he finally reached an inner resolve. Even though Brian was nearly an adult, the loss of his mother had weighed heavily on him and he had been reluctant to get close to Matthew. He also seemed to know that something was about to happen between Patricia and his father.

Although Brian had sensed the change, it came as a complete surprise to Matthew, at least at the time. After the party had broken up, he went to his study and began deliberating over a map of Taipei that Robert had left behind. Patricia, coming in from the kitchen, was carrying a tray containing two cups of coffee, cream, and sugar. She had set the tray down next to him but he was so intent on the map that he hardly noticed. Her presence, though, he felt strongly.

Seeing his neck bent over in deep thought, she

189

leaned over and kissed it. When he turned around, they smiled and embraced, nearly spilling the tray. Her kisses were direct and Matthew could feel her breasts pressed firmly against his chest. A few minutes later, they were passionately guiding each other towards the bedroom across the hall. Untouched, the coffee on the tray became cold. Until that moment, Matthew had not made love to a woman in over two years.

At ten o'clock the next morning, the ringing telephone woke them. Patricia, still sleepy, snuggled closer to Matthew's chest, making it difficult for him to reach the telephone.

"Hello?" he asked sleepily.

"I understand that you may need a chopper pilot for a little 'adventure' that you're contemplating?" the voice on the other end of the line asked.

"I... I <u>might</u> need one," Matthew responded warily. Judging from the events during the past several weeks, he could not predict what the next moment might bring.

"I'm your man," the voice responded unequivocally.

"Great! Now, who are you?"

"Sam... Sam Strickland, your expedition pilot!"

"I thought the voice sounded familiar!"

"I think you've been handed a raw deal," he continued. "I just got the word of the 'plan' this morning. I'll even chuck in twenty-thousand dollars to help make it work."

"Fair dinkum?!" Another spot of good fortune.

190

After Strickland had rung off, Matthew stretched and got up to make some breakfast. A stray beam of sunlight had escaped from the morning cloud cover and was illuminating the room brightly. For the first time in nearly two months, he was feeling good.

Although he had prepared "breakfast-in-bed" for her, Patricia insisted on getting up and joining him in the kitchen to eat it. She wore only his bathroom robe, which was too large for her and constantly left one shoulder or the other exposed. Matthew found it suggestive and arousing.

About halfway through their meal and a back rub, Brian appeared in the kitchen doorway. Solemnly, he sat down at the table and looked at them in a thoughtful manner. Matthew was still caressing Patricia's shoulders.

"Dad?"

"Yes, son?" *Here it comes*, he thought. He braced himself.

"I would like to join the recapture effort."

"Huh?" Matthew hadn't been prepared for that. "Are you sure? It could be dangerous." He was secretly delighted.

"I'm more certain of this than anything ever before," Brian assured him while rising from the table.

"Fair dinkum! son." Matthew went over and clapped his shoulders and shook his hand. "Thank you." *He's finally laid his mother to rest.*

Starting for the back door, Brian stopped and turned towards the couple with a smile.

"I like your girlfriend, Dad."

Then picking up his helmet from the cluttered table by the door, he quietly left the room.

The sputtering sound of Brian's motorcycle drifting down the driveway - instead of an angry roar - seemed to signal that he was allowing Patricia and his father the "emotional" space for their new relationship. After breakfast was over, Matthew and Patricia went back to bed. They fell together onto the sheets and into love.

Chapter Eighteen

Together, Patricia and Brian entered the huge lobby of Yeoh Chin Choo's Yellow Dragon Hotel. They were there to "case" the place out while Matthew waited in a hotel room across town. Because of the chance that Chin would recognize him, he had stayed behind.

Most of the "release" team, as Bill Schwartz called his motley group, had already arrived and were renting similar rooms down the hall from Matthew. While they were entertaining themselves by taking in the tourist sights and stuffing themselves with exotic food and beer, Matthew had elected to stay behind and pace the floor.

Am I taking this enterprise too seriously? What if we failed? Or if someone got hurt? Matthew wondered.

Patricia had called him the team's duly designated "worry wart."

I am certainly acting the part, he mused.

...

Once past the doormen guarding the lobby's grand entrance, Patricia and Brian could see the top of the Thylacines' glass cage towering above the crowded que of people waiting to catch a glimpse of these celebrity animals. They joined the line and inched forward while listening to a pretty Chinese girl explain how the animals were cared for.

"What happens if they get sick?" Brian asked casually. He already knew the answer. He had read the newspaper and magazine articles.

"We have a veterinary team, complete with operating room, only a block away. They can be here to help in less than five minutes, twenty-four hours a day."

"What do you feed these animals?" Patricia asked while taking her camera out of her bag.

"Sorry, but no pictures are allowed," the girl interjected.

Patricia glanced around, one of the security men standing near the end of the cage was looking at her. She put the camera away.

"We're just going to have to memorize every detail," she thought.

Entering the lobby, the Thylacine cage was situated in the far right-hand corner of the room. There was an information kiosk situated near the center and a check-in and reservation desk along the left wall. Against the back wall, a bank of elevators formed an impressive array of steel doors. There were also several courtesy couch and chair ensembles for guests to sit on, placed out of the flow of traffic and well away from the glass cage.

At least four "plainclothes" security guards monitored the crowd. They were fairly easy to spot because all of them wore the same sort of dark blue suit and carried a small two-way radio in their hand.

"I wonder if that bulge under that bloke's jacket

is a gun?" Brian whispered to Patricia.

"Let's assume it is and that they all are carrying," she responded. During the past few weeks of preparation and travel, she and Brian had become good friends. Right now, because of their close situation, every glance between them imparted significance.

"You're the best thing that's happened to Dad and me in years," Brian confided to her on the way back to Matthew's hotel room.

After they returned, Patricia drew a detailed sketch of the lobby for the rest of the team.

"Great! Now all we need is a route map."

"Let's get something to eat first," Brian suggested.

"Good idea," Matthew added. "Let's take Robert Tan with us; he's familiar with this city and speaks the language. We also need to go over his role in this game."

"He's crucial to our success," said Patricia. "That's why I asked him to join us."

Robert led them to a large but crowded Chinese restaurant said to be a local favorite. It must have been true; Patricia, Brian and Matthew were the only "Westerners" in the whole place.

"I hope that Mr. Yeoh doesn't see your Dad," Patricia whispered to Brian.

"Probably not much chance of that in here. He's too rich for this establishment," Robert reassured her. "Still, let's not talk too loudly. A lot of these Chinese understand English even if they don't let on that they do... so what would you like to eat?"

"We'll let you do the ordering, if you don't mind," Matthew said.

The supper was a delicious mix of seafood and vegetable dishes cooked in the middle of the table in a large gas-fired metal appliance called a "steam boat." Plates of raw food containing strips of meat, fish-balls, squid, snapper fillets, pork, and various greens were dumped into a boiling soup base and stirred. When cooked, the diners picked out individual pieces with chop-sticks and popped them into their mouths. As soon as the heated soup bowl started to become empty, it was filled with more plates of exotic food, including cutup chunks of jellyfish. It was, as Robert had promised, "a varied feast designed to last for hours."

Brian was having considerable difficulty using chopsticks. Every time he lifted a good-looking morsel to his mouth, it would fall onto the table or the floor. The group laughed and encouraged him, but it didn't help. Finally, in order to keep him from going hungry, a waiter issued him a fork and he joined in on the feast.

Robert Tan made his living as a computer consultant and specialized in data recovery from computer systems that had "crashed." A small, seemingly happy-go-lucky business man in his mid-thirties, he was unusual among the hardworking Hong Kong born immigrants in that he was also a passionate nature lover and a bird watcher. Since moving to Australia, he had became a driving force in the Victoria Nature Society which had its headquarters in Melbourne.

As he talked about his family, a wife and two lovely daughters, Matthew sensed that Patricia had indeed made a good choice in him; he seemed to be one of those rare people who was willing to go the extra mile for his friends or for something he believed in, especially if his friends believed in it too.

"Tomorrow, I will check into the Yellow Dragon," he told the group in a low tone. "When I have completed all the necessary preparations, we will meet back in your hotel room, Matthew."

After dinner, the team returned to their hotel, thanked Robert for the great dining experience and went off to their respective rooms. Patricia and Matthew shared the same bed and now regarded themselves as a couple.

"That was a fabulous dinner," Matthew said while watching her prepare for bed. "And you are a fabulous woman."

She slipped in beside him as he turned off the lights. Within a few minutes, they were both asleep in each other's arms.

Nearly a week passed before Robert called for the next meeting. During that time, Patricia, Brian, and Matthew went out together each morning to explore another portion of Taipei and its surrounding countryside. Brian, in particular, had fun finding new foods and places to eat. They also discovered that the Chinese culture was a rich tapestry whose every thread was fascinating to examine.

Matthew could not have dreamed of having a more enjoyable time with his "new" family. Although they were here to do a dangerous job that might fail in injury or imprisonment, he was happier than he had been in years.

"Finding a local who would collaborate with us was rather difficult," Robert Tan told the group assembled in Matthew's room. "After a lot subtle inquiries, I found a busboy at the hotel who could be bribed. Although it cost us thirty-five thousand dollars, I think he'll do the job. As insurance that he will do what we ask, I discovered where he lives - it's a miserable little flat - and told him that my associates in the secret society would hunt him down if he tried to skip. You've heard of our famous secret societies, haven't you?"

"Do you mean the Triad gangs?" Brian asked.

"No, these groups are far larger and more pervasive, much like the Mafia in Europe and America."

...

They were nearly ready. Troy had recently sent a radio-fax saying that he was about six hundred nautical miles off the coast of Taiwan and would probably arrive outside of Taipei in a few days. He had left Hobart with his big cruiser, *Storm Lass,* and a couple of trusted crew members two and a half weeks earlier.

Sam Strickland had found a helicopter that could be rented but he still needed to clear his flight plan with the Taiwanese authorities. Ostensibly, the story was that he was going to ferry a rich businessman from the roof of a parking garage near the Yellow Dragon to the deck of a large cruiser anchored in the harbor. This story was raising a few eyebrows and so a large chunk of the team's "buy off" money was being used to grease the slower turning wheels of this bureaucracy. Since Robert was helping in these negotiations, Sam assured the group that they would have the loose ends of their plan finalized in a day or two.

"A day or two" stretched out into nearly another week. Robert had to visit the busboy every couple of days in order to keep him from panicking. He advised the young man that he might want to move to another city as soon he had completed the job. In anticipation, Matthew was beginning to pace the floor again. Only Patricia and Brian seemed to be truly unworried. Although they practically had to drag Matthew out of the hotel to go sight-seeing every day, he soon felt better for having done so.

"He has a tendency to cloister himself when he's waiting for things to happen," Patricia explained.

It's ironical, but when everything was finally ready to go, somehow it seemed too sudden to Matthew. The team had decided to make its move on the next day, a Monday. Each weekend the Yellow Dragon became swamped with visitors and guests and during that time everyone working at the hotel became "geared up" in order to handle the increased workload.

But on Mondays, when things were relatively quiet, the hotel's staff, including Security, appeared to relax. Robert Tan felt that a strike at this moment might give them a slight advantage.

After an early dinner, the team met in Matthew's room for one last briefing. Each face displayed an eagerness that did not seem marred in the least by fear or self-doubt.

Am I the only one who is experiencing butterflies in the stomach? Matthew asked himself.

"Sam, you should go and get the helicopter now," Matthew instructed. "Troy is waiting in position offshore."

"We all know what to do... but if things go wrong, don't panic. Try to keep your head and look for options. That's the key... options."

"Any questions?" Matthew asked while standing up to signal the game had begun. There were none. They had gone over the plan so many times that everyone knew it by heart.

"Let's go!"

They filed out of the room and took the lift down to the street. Robert and Bill joined Matthew in a taxi ride that took them within two blocks of the Yellow Dragon. Then they loitered and pretended to shop while keeping an eye on the traffic around the Yellow Dragon.

Sometime during this afternoon, a Chinese busboy had slipped six capsules of ketamine hydro-chloride into the special meat kept in the walk-in locker at the back of the hotel's restaurant. He then nervously slipped out of the building and vanished into the crowded city.

At exactly 6:00 PM, a young keeper, the daughter of the veterinarian, would roll her food-laden cart out to the Thylacine pen. A guard would close an exclusion gate and open the back of the pen so she could clean it and change the bedding material. The meat - big pieces of imported kangaroo - would then be attached to long cords hanging from the ceiling of the pen. The hanging meat then would be swung, back and forth, like a pendulum.

After the girl left the cage and the dividing gate was pulled back, the Thylacines would rush in and grab the pieces of swinging meat. They had been trained to treat the swinging objects as if they were live prey.

After swallowing the affected meat, each animal would become unsteady for a few moments and then drop to the floor unconscious. This is when the alarm would go out.

Matthew looked at his watch. It was already twenty past six. He glanced over to Robert and Bill. They looked bewildered. In another hour it would be sunset and soon too dark for Sam to fly the helicopter.

Had our conspiracy failed? he wondered.

As if in answer, the undulating wail of a siren suddenly split the air when an ambulance entered the street from the veterinarian's quarters. A larger-than-usual crowd flooded the steps of the Yellow Dragon.

Matthew could imagine Chin barking orders to

201

his security guards to clear away the crush of curious people.

In a minute or two, the unconscious animals would be removed from their cage and transported, probably by litter, to the waiting ambulance. As a safety precaution, Chin would probably order a couple of guards to go with the ambulance when it pulled away.

Matthew glanced quickly across the street. Shawn and Katrina were ready with the rental car.

One...two...three...four... Here comes the ambulance, pressing its way through the crowd.

Then, just before the ambulance reached the first street intersection, Shawn gunned the car from where it was parked and drove it straight into the ambulance, ramming its right front fender. A confused gathering of onlookers quickly formed and began yelling in Chinese.

As Shawn and his girlfriend attempted to make a hurried exit on foot in different directions, one of the guards stuck his head out of the back of the ambulance. Before he could call to the crowd to stop the fleeing drivers, Robert ran up and hit him with a blackjack. He fell back into the vehicle. By the time Bill and Matthew reached the back door of the ambulance, Robert had already knocked out the other guard and was holding the driver by the collar.

Robert harangued the crowd in Chinese in an effort to divert their attention from the car's fleeing occupants and to help push the blocking vehicle out of the way. Meanwhile, Bill and Matthew stuffed the two unconscious Thylacines into large rice sacks. They had to move very fast before the crowd realized what was happening.

The police began to arrive just as they cleared away from the ambulance. While Bill and Matthew lugged the sacks around the corner, Robert vanished into the assemblage. Halfway down the block they met Brian, who was carrying two more bulging rice bags.

"Drop them on the sidewalk, son."

The bags had been filled with packing excelsior to act as decoys.

"Here, Bill give your bag to Brian and then keep on going."

Bill handed the bag he was carrying to Brian and split off, crossing the side street and entering an alley.

Shouldering their bags, Matthew and Brian turned into a large multistory parking garage. Just inside, Patricia waited in another rental car, its motor running. They placed their bags on the front seat and dove into the back. Patricia, driving, charged up the spiral ramp that led to the roof. They met only one other vehicle on the way up, but having to slow down and follow while the driver went to the next level in his search for a parking place, was nerve-wracking.

Sam and the helicopter were waiting on the roof. While Matthew and Brian loaded the Thylacines and then climbed aboard, Patricia parked the car so that it would block the entry ramp.

"Hurry!" Brian yelled when Sam began powering up for liftoff. Patricia pulled herself up into the copilot's seat and shut the cabin door. As they rose into the air, Matthew had the brief sensation that it was the roof of the parking garage that was actually moving, downward and away from them.

So far so good; we're going to make it!

A few moments earlier, a policeman had discovered the two bags that Brian had dropped. When he yelled for help in opening them, another policeman and several of Chin's security guards ran over to assist. It took a only few seconds before they realized that the dummy Thylacines were fakes. Then they heard the sound of the helicopter taking off.

Just as it was clearing the building, one of the security men backed out into the street and pulled out a revolver. As he aimed it at the aircraft, a policeman saw what was happening and tackled the guard while yelling, "You don't know who is in that helicopter!"

They both tumbled into a heap... only a fraction of a second after the shot was fired. Perhaps the policeman's act of hitting the guard had actually caused him to shoot, no one really knows.

Matthew <u>did</u> know that the bullet ripped through the floor of the helicopter and through the calf of his left leg, finally lodging itself into the ceiling. With no vital parts damaged, however, the helicopter continued to gain altitude and speed, heading out to sea.

Brian tore open his father's pant-leg and

attempted to staunch the flow of blood, which dripped all over the two motionless sacks lying on the floor.

"Here!" Patricia cried. "Use my scarf to help bind the wound." She was beginning to sob.

"Steady on, girl, I'll be okay," Matthew assured her. She couldn't hear him above the noise of the chopper but apparently she had read his face, because she smiled weakly back.

Matthew's leg started to throb with searing pain, even as the bleeding abated. He was lucky in that it was a short clean wound from a small caliber bullet and probably would leave no permanent damage.

Even though the bleeding from his leg was nearly stopped, one of the sacks containing the Thylacines seemed to be getting progressively bloodier.

"Let me have a look at that bag, Dad," yelled Brian as he bent over and grabbed the sack. Pulling it past Matthew's legs, he lifted it upon his lap and untied the opening. The Thylacine inside still appeared to be asleep. It was also covered with blood.

"Dad! I think this animal has been hit by a bullet."

Matthew passed his hand into the sack and ran it along the sleeping animal's body. His fingertips found the moist and ragged wound where the bullet had passed through and exited its side. Without a sound, the animal shivered beneath his touch and then lay still.

He knew that it had died. Matthew shook his head slowly at Brian's questioning stare. Then Brian leaned his head into his father's shoulder.

"I'm sorry, Dad, I'm sorry."

...

In the glow of the last light of day, Sam located Troy's big boat and hovered above it.

"Brian, there's a coiled line under the front passenger seat. Tie one of those sacks to a rope end, and we'll lower it down to the deck. Okay, mate?" yelled Sam above the noise of the engine.

Brian nodded assent and reached forward, locating the rope. After tying the bundle, he looked up at Sam for further instructions.

"Okay, sweetheart," he said to Patricia, "open your door and lift it off its hing-pins."

Patricia opened the door and yanked upward. It came away so easily that she nearly fell out of the aircraft.

Sam swung the helicopter towards the right. "Drop the door into the sea," he shouted. Patricia let go of the door and watched it splash. It immediately began to sink.

Hovering back over the boat again, Sam nodded towards Brian. The bundle was lowered through the space between the skids and the airframe. Troy and his crew easily snagged the line with a boat hook and guided its descent into their waiting hands. Both bags are successfully lowered in this way.

"Okay!" Sam yelled, "time to go swimming!"

He swung the helicopter about twenty metres

away from the port side of the boat and lowered it until it was only three metres above the water's surface.

"Good thing there's no breeze or chop," he said, to no one in particular.

"Okay, Patricia, your turn!"

Patricia shot Matthew a terrified glance.

"It's okay!" he hollered and waved her on.

Unbuckling her seat harness, she gingerly stepped down to the skid, stood there looking determined for one long moment and then she dropped away into the sea. The sudden loss of weight on that side of the aircraft caused the helicopter to lurch abruptly but Sam quickly got it back under control.

"You're next, mate," he said indicating Brian with his index finger. "Push the seat forward and climb past it."

Brian did as he was told.

"Okay! Hold on for a minute," Sam instructed Brian when he had climbed halfway out of the cockpit. "You're going to have to slide over to the other side, Matthew. Are you up to it?"

Matthew nodded and slid into Brian's old position. The injured leg shot fathoms of pain into his being.

Rotten luck.

Brian made the jump and quickly swam over to the boat. Again the helicopter bucked and swayed for a moment until Sam brought it back under control.

"All right, Matthew, it's just you and me. Want to go back to Taipei with me and face the music?... or try swimming and hope that blood doesn't attract any sharks?"

"Get me in as close as you can, I'll try swimming."

"Right-o! Bind that leg as best you can," Sam suggested. Then reaching in the pocket of his wind-breaker, he pulled out the little wooden carving that Matthew had given him way back in base camp.

Seeing his surprised face, Sam smiled and said, "You're going to need all the luck you can get, mate."

He shoved it into Matthew's shirt pocket, buttoned the flap over it, then nodded for him to get going.

"Be careful when you step onto the skid!" he hollered as Matthew's footing momentarily slipped out from under him.

Hanging on only by his hands, Matthew looked down and saw that he had a clear opening to drop through, then he let go. Simultaneously, at the moment he hit the water, Sam lifted the helicopter away and Brian dove back into the sea from the stern of the cruiser. Within a few seconds he was by his father's side.

"Do you need help, Dad?"

"No, I don't think so. My leg actually feels a bit better floating in the water."

Wary of sharks, they swam together over to the boat. Luckily, none appeared. When Matthew had trouble mounting the boarding ladder, Troy and his big-muscled crew literally lifted him the rest of the way aboard. For a few moments he lay on the deck panting, then managed to pull himself up into a sitting position. The woodcarving was still stuck in his pocket.

With the light fading fast, Sam turned the helicopter back towards the island of Taiwan and clattered away into the distance. Much to everyone's surprise, a few minutes later he returned and hovered off the vessel's stern.

Turning on the deck lights, Troy stopped the boat's engines and leaned out of the pilot house.

"What's going on?" Brian called to him.

"Sam telephoned me over the radio, mate... it looks like he wants to join us for supper."

"What?!" Patricia and Matthew cried in unison. All hands came on deck to watch as Sam detached the pilot's door and let it, too, fall into the sea. Then he moved the helicopter about one-hundred and fifty metres away from the starboard side of the boat and hovered again. He could be seen inside, silhouetted against the evening sky. Matthew knew this was going to be an extremely tricky maneuver.

Flying a helicopter is difficult enough, but it takes real skill for a pilot to bail out of one without getting injured or killed. The tensioners on the collective controls must be tightened to the maximum by hand so that the stick will stay in whatever position the pilot leaves it in. Once the controls are set, he will have only a few seconds to exit the aircraft before it loses stability.

Sam was now standing on the runner, with his

right hand still on the controls. The helicopter was only about five metres above the surface of the sea.

A moment later, a large man-shaped object fell through the narrow strip of light between the aircraft and the horizon. Immediately, the pilotless helicopter lurched violently to the right, flying sideways and downward until it, too, hit the water.

"Everybody get down!" the skipper yelled. Most of the people on deck were already down.

The impact of the whirling blades hitting the water caused them to shatter explosively, destroying the entire aircraft. Bits of flying debris shot skyward and a flash of fire erupted briefly. One of the boat's radio antennas was severed by a piece of shrapnel, then the helicopter was gone and all was quiet. The onlookers were stunned by the sudden ending.

"Hey, you blokes! How about a hand getting into the boat?" called a voice near the boat.

They had momentarily forgotten about Sam out there, swimming in the near darkness. Everyone rushed toward the stern of the vessel, but Matthew's injury prevented him from taking more than a couple of steps. Brian threw a life-ring tied to a line, which Sam gratefully put his arm into. Then the crew quickly pulled him to the boat and helped him up the boarding ladder.

"Well, there goes our insurance deposit on the chopper," Sam quipped humorously. "Beats going to the slammer, though. I reckoned that Taiwanese mob would want to ask a whale of a lot of questions if

I went back to return their machine. Anyone got a beer?"

A can of "VB" materialized, seemingly out of thin air.

"Good on ya, mate," he told the crewman who handed it to him.

While Sam sipped the beer and stripped to dry himself off, the boat was gotten back underway, headed in a southerly direction with its running lights turned off. The undulating sea, humped with long glassy swells, made the vessel rise and fall but did nothing to slow its progress.

Chapter Nineteen

The team's dinner that night was not filled with camaraderie and laugher. They had buried the dead Thylacine at sea by weighting its bag with an iron bar and a spare hammer that were found in the tool locker. Although the body vanished the instant that it fell into the water, they stood for nearly ten minutes in reverie, staring into the breast of the gentle swell. The male Thylacine was gone, but at least a female of his kind was still alive. Perhaps there was even a chance that she might be pregnant?

Placed into a holding pen that had been specially built to protect its occupants from the wind and weather, the female soon recovered from the drug that had caused her deathlike trance. However, without the presence of her mate, she seemed subdued and refused to eat any of the wallaby meat that was being stored in the ship's freezer.

Unable to sleep, Matthew sat on the ship's bridge and watched a hazy dawn slowly overcome the night. Patricia brought him breakfast, then nursed his wound. After putting on clean bandages, she helped him to painfully lie down on the daybed to rest and, hopefully, get some sleep. His leg had become stiff and was nearly useless.

...

It was midday when Matthew woke.

Apparently, no one had pursued their escape from Taiwan.

"How is the female doing?" he asked Troy, who was at the helm.

"Still not eating... won't even drink any water," he replied shaking his head.

All that day and into the following one, the misty sky slowly coalesced into pans of streaked clouds that soon formed serrated ranks marching across the horizon. A brisk wind eliminated the sea's glassy appearance, replacing it with a white-capped chop that shook the boat. Looking up from his bed, Matthew noticed Troy and a crewman poring over a chart. Brian was at the wheel.

"G'day, Dad. You've been asleep for bloody hours. You hungry?"

"Yes I am, mate. Thirsty, too. Is our Thylacine doing any better?"

"Not yet, Dad. Patricia says she still won't eat or drink. She seems to be gettin' sick."

"Well, maybe she's seasick," suggested Troy. He pushed firm a loose pin that helped hold the chart flat on the table. "There's a storm brewing up ahead which I don't think we can outrun or otherwise avoid. Things might get a bit sloppy before we're through it. What do you reckon, Matthew? You up to this?"

"You're the skipper, mate. Just let me ride it out here in the wheel house with you... I'd prefer to see what's happening rather than be holed up in some stateroom lying on a bunk."

Over the next several hours the seas became progressively more and more uncomfortable. Brian, who was becoming seasick, was replaced by an experienced crewman. The shudder and roll of the boat, pitched by a quartering sea was also taking its toll on Matthew. Although he rarely got seasick, his leg throbbed with pain on every downward plunge of the bow. A darkening band across the horizon ahead indicated that they were approaching the storm front. Matthew began to prepare himself for the searing pain that was sure to follow.

Rain often accompanies tropical storms. It is a peculiar rain, not the wind-lashed drizzle one encounters in temperate latitudes, but a drenching, all encompassing phenomena that can flatten waves and reduce visibility to just a few feet. It is so intense that it will find its way into the tightest vessel as seeps around doorway fittings and drips around the window seals. Shafts of lightning periodically split the dark air and the following explosions of thunder shake you into realizing just how fragile our existence really is. It is as if all the world was just a toy for the gods to play with. Then, just as suddenly as it began, the rain stops, the sky lightens, the forgotten wind freshens, and whitecaps appear once more.

...

Hours turned into days as the boat continued its long plodding journey back to Tasmania. During that time, two positive events helped bolster the team's spirits. Matthew's leg began to heal without infection and the Thylacine accepted her first meal. Soon, both the Thylacine and Matthew were appearing healthy again. He could even make his way around the boat if he moved carefully, but his leg still hurt if it was bumped even the slightest.

They reached their destination at Sandy Cape, situated halfway between Mount Hazelton and Mount Norfolk on the northwest coast of Tasmania in a little more than two weeks after leaving Taipei. Only once during the entire four-thousand and three-hundred mile voyage did they put into port for fuel and supplies. Troy had chosen Cairns, that rough and tumble city at the northern end of Australia's great Pacific Highway, for his port of call.

In order to attract as little attention as possible before they entered harbor, the team moved the Thylacine into a carrying cage and dismantled the animal enclosure on the deck. It was reassembled in Brian's stateroom after the furniture had been moved out. Although it was a tight fit, it would keep the transferred animal out of sight from inquisitive port officials.

Luckily, their arrival at the Cairns fuel dock was casual and went practically unnoticed. In fact, it took them nearly thirty minutes to find the fuel-pump attendant in order to fill the boat's tanks. Since Troy had installed his own water desalinization system on board, there was no need to ship fresh water. Just three hours after docking, they were ready to be on their way

216

again.

During their short time in harbor, Patricia and the ship's cook practically cleaned out the local grocery. Matthew had prudently stayed on board and played small stakes poker with Brian and the remaining crew. He had lost nearly every round.

...

As they lowered the transfer cage containing the Thylacine down to the dinghy, heavy drops of rain began to spatter the boat's deck and the shoulders of the swells passing under them. Above the sea and the nearby beach, a mantle of swirling fog created a mysterious shroud over the tops of the mountains along this remote stretch of Tasmanian coast.

According to a recent magazine article that Matthew had read, more "Tiger" sightings have been reported from this region than from all of the rest of Tasmania put together. In any case, it would soon be the new home for this Thylacine; hopefully, she would not live the rest of her life alone in these Alps.

Already on shore, Patricia and Brian sat on a driftwood log, impatiently waiting to help carry the cage from the skiff when it landed on the beach.

"I must go ashore, too. I have to go with that cage until the end!" Matthew told himself.

At first, Troy attempted to prevent him from joining the crewman in the dinghy. After one look at his determined face, however, he backed off and helped him climb down into the boat.

Matthew was so excited by the anticipation of their long odyssey being almost finished that he hardly felt the cramp and pain coursing through his leg. With a wave, Troy summoned his crew out of the boat and then came down and took up the oars himself. He smiled at Matthew knowingly, who closed his eyes, took a deep breath, and shoved off.

This is the right thing to do.

When they landed, Troy and Matthew lifted opposite ends of the cage and staggered up the beach with it. Brian and Patricia ran down to help them.

"What are you doing here?" Patricia snapped. "That leg is not healed yet."

"I want to help release the Thylacine. It's important to me."

"Think your leg can hold up, Dad?" Brian asked in concern.

"It will have to," Matthew responded, trying to sound tough. Then added, "I just hope that I don't have to be carried back to the boat."

They set the cage down on the upper beach and reconnoitered for a game trail or some route that would penetrate the forest and lead them up the hill. A gully formed by a creek that ran down the beach looked like a good starting point.

"Are we ready?" Matthew asked. The three determined faces that looked back at him told him that they were. Glancing down at the Thylacine, he noticed that it seemed to have perked up some.

"She smells fresh food," Brian suggested.

"Or another Thylacine," Patricia offered.

Troy pulled out a VHF handheld radio and spoke into it. "*Storm Lass, Storm Lass*, this is your Skipper. Please withdraw two or three nautical miles offshore and standby for my next call. See you in a few hours, guys. Troy, out."

The big boat responded by blowing its horn and turning towards sea. Slowly, it began to move away.

"Well, the four of us ought to be able to knock this job over in a hurry, don't you reckon, Matthew?" Troy asked as he turned back towards the group, smiling humorously.

"Thanks, it's good to have you along," Patricia agreed smiling at Matthew.

Another drenching rain shower began just as they simultaneously took up a corner of the cage and began heading up the beach towards the watercourse mentioned earlier. With four of them carrying the cage, the going was fairly easy... except where the passage became narrow and they had to proceed in single file.

As the rain continued to pelt them, the ground became more soggy and treacherous to walk on. Brian lost his footing and smacked his chin on the limb of a snow gum. It began to bleed profusely.

"Let's take a break," Matthew told the group. Their clothes were becoming sopping wet, matted hair hung in front of Patricia's face.

"I think we're about halfway up to the top of the ridge," he said.

Again, they stood and lifted the cage together.

219

In response, the mists seemed to close ever tighter into the surrounding forest and the rain drops increased their size. Matthew was beginning to shiver from the chill, when his feet suddenly went out from under him and he found himself sliding on his back, down and into the trunk of a tree. The impact of the crash knocked the wind out of him and, for a while, he lay there stunned.

"Are you all right?" Troy called. Matthew didn't answer.

"Dad!"

They put the cage down and made their way to where he lay. With helping hands he managed to sit up. Glancing down at his leg, Brian noticed a large dark red patch of blood staining his father's pant leg.

"Damn," Matthew said gritting his teeth. "I've opened the wound again. Anyone got a belt or a scarf I could borrow?"

Troy removed his belt and offered it to him. After cinching it around his leg to staunch the flow of blood, he felt strong enough to crawl to his feet. His wet and muddy clothes were a mess... so was everyone else's.

It's not much further to the top.

Shouldering the cage again, they managed to carry it until they reached a spot just below the top of the ridge. Here, as the bedrock broke out above the tree-line, Troy stumbled. As if on cue, everyone else lost their hold on the Thylacine cage, allowing it to crash to the ground and slide to the very edge of a small precipice. Oddly, instead of becoming agitated, the

220

Thylacine inside stayed calm, seemingly taking the incident in her stride.

The rain stopped just as the group reached the top of the dividing ridge and set the cage down on a spot that offered a few square metres of flat ground. Matthew was so exhausted that he immediately sat down. Brian and Patricia did the same on either side of him. They each put an arm around his shoulders, propping him up from both sides. Troy remained standing and peered over the far edge of the ridge. The valley below was completely obscured by fog.

Then a break in the cloud cover allowed the sun to shine low over the fog bank, illuminating it with a golden glow that seemed to come from within.

Troy looked back at the huddled little band and asked, "Shall we open the cage now?"

Matthew nodded his consent.

After the cage door was opened, the Thylacine stiffly, and with almost hesitating reluctance, stepped out into freedom. After a few moments, it trotted off, stopping part way down the steep slope to look back at the small group of people. Then it turned and disappeared into the glowing mist.

A sob shook Matthew's shoulder and he turned his head and saw that Patricia was crying.

"Good-bye and farewell," she grieved. "I... I hope you are not the last of your... of your... kind." She choked as she finished the last word.

Brian's eyes were welling with tears, too. Reaching into a pocket in his jacket, Matthew withdrew the carved wooden amulet that Sam had given back to him. After fingering it for a moment, he noticed that Patricia was smiling weakly. He smiled back and struggled to stand up. Six willing hands helped him to his feet.

After staggering a few steps towards edge of the ridge, Matthew threw the wooden charm out into the fog and down into the valley that the Thylacine had disappeared into.

"You'll need all the luck that you can get, little mate," he called after it.

As they stood on the ridge-top, silently listening and staring at the fog, the mist cleared momentarily, revealing a rocky outcrop far below. On the rock stood the Thylacine, alone, calm, gazing back at them with those quiet eyes. Then the haze closed in around her and she disappeared from their view forever.

*

Glossary of Selected
Australian
and
Technical Terms

Abseiling = A method of descending a sheer cliff face by means of a rope arranged around one's body so that the slide can be controlled.

Beer = Preferred drinking fluid of most Australian men.

Bugger all = Commonly heard oath when beer is not available.

Bundaburg rum = <u>The</u> Australian rum.

Bundy = Same rum, shorter name.

Big Apple = aka New York. (See listing for New York)

Billy tea = Tea boiled in a fire-blackened kettle flavored with a bit of wood ash and dirt. Yum!

Bloke = Man, Male person.

Bushy = Woodsman, outdoorsman.

Carnassial teeth = The "cheek" teeth of a predator that allow it to bite off chunks of meat from a carcass.

Centimetre = Mysterious measurement of less than a half an inch.

Chimneying = A technique of climbing a deep narrow fissure in a cliff, often by alternately bracing one's feet on one side and sliding one's butt up the other.

Cirque = A natural amphitheater. (Steep hollow excavation in a mountain made by erosion)

CITES = Convention on International Trade in
        Endangered Species.

Cupper = Cup of coffee or tea.

Damper bread = Campfire bread, sometimes quite
        tasty, especially if you have been
        several days without food.

Eucalyptus = Ubiquitous tree of Australia

Fair dinkum = "The real thing." (Not Coke)

Flat = What many animals who try to cross a highway
        end up being. Also, a city apartment.

Fortnight = Period of two weeks.

Glacial till = Gravel and soil left behind by a receding
        glacier.

Grub = Food.

Hessian = Burlap.

Hide = A blind or structure to conceal one's self in.

Ketamine hydrocloride = Knockout drops.

Kilometre = Another mysterious distance measurement
        usually 0.6 of a mile, but in outback
        Australia can vary anywhere from 0.1 to
        120 miles.

Mate = Friend. (Best mate = Best friend)

Metre = Another length measurement equaling about a
        yard or so.

New York = Geographic center of the Civilized World.

No worries = Mindless Australian expression meaning
        "Not a problem".

Panchax = A real fish kept by aquarists.

Platypus = Weird but loveable Australian animal.

Potoroo = Another weird but loveable Aussie critter.

Rosella = Small, noisy, but loveable Australian parrot.

Scree = An accumulation of small broken stones often found at the foot of steep slopes.

Smoko = Work break which can vary from 10 minutes to 10 hours.

Solicitor = A nice name for a lawyer. The rest are unprintable.

Swag = A portable outdoor bed consisting of a rolled up mat and blankets.

Torch = Flashlight.

Tea = Dinner. (Also, something to drink between beers or while at work)

Tea-time = Dinner-time.

Telly = Television.

Trammel-net = Tangle net for catching wildlife.

Tucker = Another word for food.

Thylacine = What this book is all about.

UNESCO = United Nations Educational, Scientific and Cultural Organization.

VB = Beer. (aka Victoria Bitters)

Vittles = Yet another word for food.

Wallaby = Small kangaroo (Usually less than 21 pounds in weight)

Wewak = A small town in Papua New Guinea. (Charming spot but the mosquitos here transmit Dengue fever and Malaria. Good place for most tourists to avoid.)

Yank = Any US citizen found outside the borders of the United States.